The Max Chronicles Presents

The STORY TELLER 1

Ernie Carwile

The Max Chronicles Presents

The STORY TELLER 1

Ernie Carwile

Verbena Pond Publishing Co., LLC

2008   2007   2006   2005   2 3 4 5

ISBN: 0-9752854-0-8
LCCN 2004103434

Chapter 5 contains a selection from *The Prophet* by Kahlil Gibran, copyright 1923 by Kahlil Gibran and renewed 1951 by Administrators C.T.A. of Kahlil Gibran Estate and Mary G. Gibran. Used by permission of Alfred A. Knopf, a division of Random House, Inc.

*This book is dedicated to all the writers
who came before me, especially those
who continue speaking through me.*

ACKNOWLEDGEMENTS

I would prefer to always work alone, though some of my varied occupations prevented this. Writing, I initially believed, would finally allow me this option. This belief proved to be dead wrong.

Anyone who has ever published a book already knows that for it to become a reality, many others contribute.

I especially want to thank my wife, Mary, for her persistence in helping me see my errors, her insightful suggestions and loving support; my daughter, Kate, for her tactful and poignant suggestions, and total support; my editor, Jeff Mlady, for not only his editing expertise but also for lending even more support and encouragement; Joyce Miller, for her invaluable research and editing; and my friend, Cathy Shuster, for her typing, honesty, enthusiasm and energy.

AUTHOR'S NOTE

Using a parable as his medium, a good storyteller can convey a spiritual truth through real-life situations in a way that makes the truth discernible and powerful. Parables are really coded stories for the soul. Why? Because they speak to the non-physical part of who we are. Jesus once said, "I will open my mouth in parables, I will utter things hidden since the creation of the world."

Parables are really worldly stories with ethereal meanings. Their applications are universal. Whatever their cultural or historical origins, they tend to be contemporary in any time period and meaningful to any culture.

This observation proved to be a catalyst for me to begin a journey in which I started to collect the finest of the contemporary parables I encountered as well as to hone my skills at writing parables of my own modeled after them.

The Bible is not the exclusive domain for parables. The truth is they are interwoven into the fabric of societies through books, movies, family stories, rites and traditions. Wonderful parables can be found in the American Indian, Hindu and Greek cultures for example. This book contains parables I have written as well as parables from various cultures and time periods including our own.

*Be transformed by
the renewal of
your mind.*

—St. Paul

CHAPTER ONE
Attitude

Max was something to see.

Wherever he went, you'd soon find him surrounded by people, all intently listening, all savoring his words like a rich, hot fudge sundae. You could see it on their faces.

How he garnered such crowds remains a mystery. Certainly not his stature, for when standing his head usually only reached most people's nose. Nor was it his thin, wiry body, for he was rather scrawny looking, especially with his three-day, gray-white speckled beard. His demeanor seemed shy, withdrawn.

Yes, his body probably looked like any other old man's body: wizened, used up. But his energetic, fluid movements were more of a young man's, and seemed incongruent with the rest of him.

Then came the eyes: intense, burning brightly, they gave off the kind of electricity seen only in tropical thunderstorms.

I watched him do it over and over, never believing the speed at which the people became corralled, then enthralled, ensconced in his aura. There'd only be a side comment, a murmur of some words, and unaware, they'd be drawn into his spell, then entertained beyond their wildest expectations.

All through just a story. A tale. Words intricately woven together like a Hopi Indian blanket, symphonic voice inflections, pauses held just the right length, head movements accenting the most important, eyebrows raised and lowered for emphasis, eyes projecting like a movie theater.

Laughing. Frowning. Sighing. Crying. He was the master. He was the storyteller.

MARCH 18, 1998

Every so often, though rarely, someone enters your life and profoundly changes you to the very core.

This is the story of Maxwell Winston Stone, an ordinary man. His life began filled with much difficulty, but through the gift of reading, he changed the course his life was headed. Because of our friendship, I was blessed with the opportunity to observe his radical transformation—one so beyond rationality I had trouble believing, as you will too. No human being has the right to become as he did, I think . . . but I'm getting ahead of myself.

I first met Max on a foggy, cold, mystical evening, almost like something out of a Sherlock Holmes movie. The day I met Max my life was in shambles.

Think of the worst day in your life. This was mine. Nothing, and I mean nothing, was working right.

My relationship with Jenny, my wife, was falling apart. Our sex life was almost nonexistent. Our communication even worse. We were like two very polite people trying to coexist in the same space.

Money. I had been barely eking out a living in real estate. After spending all my effort and nearly all our funds on a complicated deal, I'd come to a dead end on where to take it next. Funds extremely low, bills were now paid on a priority-system basis only.

I'd read somewhere that sex, money and lack of communication were the three main killers in relationships, and my life could have been a poster example of what not to do.

And to top it all off, my car broke down. I don't know about you, but when anything mechanical goes wrong, I feel as if the universe has singled me out for special punishment.

Remember that old humorous radio sketch where the guy says, "Is your life in the toilet? Does your wife hate you? Do your kids ignore you? Does your boss want to fire you? Well, then buck up, Bucky."

I knew I had to buck up. I just didn't know how I was going to do it.

The only thing good about the car breaking down was that it did so near this neighborhood bar I'd driven by but never entered. After calling AAA and hearing there'd be a two-hour wait before a truck could get there, I heavily trod into the establishment feeling as hopeless, helpless and dejected as I'd ever felt in my life.

The place was gorgeous. A thick, dark, rich mahogany bar ran along the back left portion of the cozy room. Against the front left wall were two well-used dartboards, both occupied by obviously serious players. Groans and shouts of elation echoed from them. To the right of the bar, recessed deep into the back wall, stood a huge fireplace. Its blazing logs radiated a welcome warmth, and a grouping of soft, deep-seated, well-used leather chairs and couches surrounded it.

Here I encountered him—encircled by seven men and women, all spellbound, all intently listening to his mesmerizing words.

I approached, and almost synchronistically one of the chairs opened up as Max's story concluded. The man who got up was apologizing profusely for having to pick up one of his kids from basketball practice. I sat down.

Max nodded, I guess to make me feel welcome, but then continued staring directly into my eyes with a strange familiarity. Feeling uncomfortable, I was rescued by the waitress and asked her for something strong and warm. My attention returned. Max smiled softly, gazed momentarily at the fire and began anew.

I was amazed at the attention everyone gave this diminutive man—each of them totally enthralled. His sparkling, hypnotic eyes focused on mine as if reading on some deeper level. He didn't know me from Adam, and he certainly had no idea of my struggles at the office. So to say that Max's story surprised me was a vast understatement.

"You know," Max began, "it's easy to give up today. I remember working for this one corporation that had merged with so many other companies that it became huge and powerful. It seemed invincible, especially if you were just a little guy starting out. Competitors must have felt simply overwhelmed at the thought of even competing against this giant. I imagine many went home and pulled the covers up over their eyes.

"But you know, whenever I feel that way now, I remember a story about a Chinese family who had a store in New York City, right in Manhattan. Their family had owned it for over seventy years. It wasn't a big store, but it had been in the family for four generations by then.

"Well, one day a richly dressed, very confident man entered their store and offered to buy it. He explained they were purchasing the entire block to develop a huge department store and just needed their little store to complete the whole deal.

"Very humbly, the Chinese man responded that the store wasn't for sale, that it had belonged to his great-grandfather, then his grandfather, his father, and now it was his.

"Someday, he said, he wanted to pass it on to his own son.

"Of course the rich man became upset and offered even more money, only to be turned down again and again.

"Angrily departing, the developer gathered together with others in his company to strategize and develop a plan of attack. What they eventually decided was to build their huge store on all three sides around the little store and literally squeeze them out of business.

"The day of the big grand opening came. Following

their plan to destroy the Chinese family's little store, the developers hung two giant banners on either side of the small store. The banner on the left side read, 'Grand Opening.' The banner on the right side also said, 'Grand Opening,' thus leaving the little store completely dwarfed on all sides by the huge department store.

"At first, of course the Chinese man panicked. He realized that the developers just might succeed in squeezing him out of business.

"But, instead of giving up, he brainstormed with his family, and do you know what he came up with?" Max asked, pausing long enough to check each listener's eyes, ensuring they were awaiting his surprise. Laughing, he explained, "That little fellow went out and got a banner of his own.

"Now remember," Max reminded, "on both sides of the little store hung banners announcing 'Grand Opening.'

"Well, what the Chinese fellow did, right smack dab in the middle of those two big banners, was to hang his own."

Pausing, openly amused, Max chuckled, then delivered the finale. "It said, 'Main Entrance.' Their sales doubled in the first week. . . all from a simple change of perspective."

I remember laughing along with everyone else in our little group, pleased and entertained until it hit me like a thunderbolt. Through an explosion of insight, I received the solution to my business predicament. Snap! Just like that the answer appeared.

His story helped me immensely, and because of it I made my first real money. All from a change of attitude, from seeing the same situation from a different angle. All from Max's little tale.

By 9:30 p.m. everyone else had left except Max and me. I moved to a seat next to him, bought us each another drink and began the usual male-bonding process.

"Well, are you a Bronco fan?" I unenthusiastically inquired.

He grinned, "Oh, you bet. Saturdays are spent watching college football. Sundays, Mondays and Thursdays on the pros."

"Do you get much grief from your wife?" I sheepishly asked.

"Nope, not lucky enough to have a wife, so nobody gives me any grief, or love either." He laughed then asked, "Does your wife really mind you watching so much?"

I paused before responding. "Actually, not too much, as long as the rest of things are going okay."

We both took a swallow of our drinks, and I felt uneasy with the silence that followed. I was rethinking how odd it was men only talk about superficial stuff. Then I realized I didn't even know how to go deeper . . . or maybe I was just too insecure to do so.

I looked up at Max and saw him comfortably smiling at me, a twinkle in his eyes. "Look, it's time for this old man to go to bed, but maybe we could meet another time, and get to know one another better?"

I quickly inserted, "Hey, I'd like that," really thinking we never would.

We exchanged telephone numbers and shook hands. Max walked home while I called a taxi. The time had flown by, and AAA had towed my car off to be repaired.

✳ ✳ ✳

APRIL 9, 1998

I ran into Max again a couple weeks later at our bar and found out more about him. Just slightly slurring his words, he opened up through the alcohol, something I sensed he rarely did.

He shared the great variety of different vocations he'd had in his seventy-three years. "I was either cursed or blessed with the need to change jobs every six or seven years," he chuckled.

"Like what?" I asked.

Musing while sipping his drink, he began listing: "Paperboy, grocery sacker for tips, mechanic, librarian, lightweight boxer. Hey, I even used to drive one of those huge, huge loader trucks for Peabody Coal Mine. Why, they were so big it took six steps just to get to the driver's seat."

"Oh, come on Max, the truck wasn't that big!"

"You bet it was. In fact," his eyes searched the size of the bar, "the truck was about half the width of the whole bar and twice as tall."

"Wow, did it scare you?"

"Let's just say the first week I sweated like a pig even though the temperature was only in the forties.

"What about you?" Max switched gears.

"After college I got married and then was commissioned into the Air Force. Stayed in only two and a half years. When the Vietnam thing was winding down, I got an early out . . . dabbled in the stock market until I got burned, so I began experimenting with real estate . . . made a little money—just enough to get us by . . . But it was your story on the night we met that brought me my big break."

"My little story?" Max modestly asked.

"Definitely. After that story, or because of that story, I made my first killing. I was able to get a quick rezoning because of a technicality in the earlier, already accepted, planned unit development. Everyone else had simply missed it. Neither my wife nor I had ever seen that much money before. By the way, thanks," I said while touching my glass to his.

"You know what?" Max mumbled, his eyelids heavy, "I'm tired . . . think I'll go home . . . but why don't we meet here again in a couple weeks? Say Thursday night?"

"I'd like that Max. Have a good evening."

✳   ✳   ✳

APRIL 25, 1998

"What's your full name, Max?"

We were once again seated on barstools at our neighborhood bar.

He looked up with a small wistful smile and said, "Maxwell Winston Stone."

"Wow! That's unusual. How were you named?"

His facial expression shifted quickly, no longer amusement in his voice.

"Well, I guess Maxwell came from all the coffee my folks drank. The Winston from all the cigarettes they smoked. And Stone . . . I guess that reflected what their hearts were made of."

You could feel his mood shift, making the room's atmosphere turn heavy, thick, sad.

I've always been uncomfortable with sharing vulnerable things with other men, so I waited what I thought was an appropriate time, then asked after clearing my throat, "I know you like football . . . what about the Denver Nuggets?"

He paused awhile before responding. When he next spoke, I sensed a bit of disappointment as to the direction I had moved our conversation, or maybe I felt it was my own guilt over my lack of courage in sharing more deeply with another man.

Finally he said, "Not much on basketball. Baseball either."

Shortly thereafter we parted.

On my drive home I couldn't help replaying my cowardice in changing subjects. Next time, I pledged to myself, I would go deeper.

When I finally arrived home, I could hear my wife Jenny's soft snoring. I undressed in the bathroom, then quietly slipped into bed, feeling her warmth.

❋ ❋ ❋

JUNE 14, 1998

I received a call from Max, out of the blue, inviting me to a picnic. I accepted. We drove to Washington Park on a gorgeous Denver afternoon, both appreciating the soft, early summer sights and smells. Renowned for its beauty and size, the park contained magnificent flower gardens, towering pine and maple trees, lakes, tennis and volleyball courts, soccer and softball fields, playgrounds, a boathouse and even an old band pavilion.

On the drive over, I initiated the conversation. "Hey Max," I said with a slight smile hinting what my words might be, "I promise not to do the male thing—you know, talk about football—if you won't."

Out of the corner of my eye I saw him smile, then heard a chuckle. "Damn," he said, "I'd hoped you'd see that too! . . . I don't know why we men keep ourselves hidden from each other. It's no wonder most of us have so few real friends."

"I'm new at this," I offered, my voice expressing fear as I sensed I was moving into unknown territory. "But I'd like to go further . . . or deeper . . . or hell, I don't know how to even describe it."

Max stayed silent while I stayed uncomfortable with my admission. Fortunately he soon followed, "I know what you mean. I'd like us to get to know one another better too . . . actually I'm hoping we might become friends. I've got lots of acquaintances, but only a couple of real friends . . . how about you?"

I shook my head in confession. "I'm embarrassed to admit, but I guess I really don't have any . . . some acquaintances, but I've always stayed pretty well protected." I turned to see his response.

Eyes twinkling, he affirmed, "Then it's settled. You and I are going to become good friends." He laughed outright. "The first time I saw you I sensed maybe we could!"

We had picked up fried chicken, mashed potatoes, gravy and biscuits, along with iced-down Dr Pepper and quickly wolfed them down.

We ended our scrumptious lunch by devouring a couple of Susie-Q's, that delicious little dessert which has a shelf life of something like ninety-nine years.

Wiping the last remains of gooey concoction off his mouth, he spoke. "You've heard Einstein's statement that we use only seven percent of our brains, haven't you?"

"Yes," I replied, "and geniuses use only nine to ten percent."

Nodding his head in agreement, he continued. "That means we're not using as much as ninety percent of our brain power."

"Maybe that's why our world is in such a sad condition," I volunteered.

"I've been thinking a lot about this recently," Max said, "and I've been wondering, that if it became possible to tap into this ninety percent non-usage, what areas of the brain would it involve? How would it affect the world as we know it?"

"Those . . . are . . . great . . . questions!" I exclaimed.

"I mean," Max continued, "if you look at our world as it is today, we are seeing a planet reaching its maximum limits in areas of population growth, fossil energies, as well as food and water shortages . . . It's easy to see the areas still left to explore: the oceans and space. Yet we're limited here by lack of technology."

I nodded I was following.

"The one area to explore that is pretty much passed over . . . the one that just might contain solutions to all our problems, is the one inside us . . . accessed in the areas of the brain we've left untouched, unused and ignored."

"Max, this is fascinating."

"How about a little free thinking?" Max's eyes shone brightly. "Let's guess the problems we might be able to solve if we could use much more of our brain."

"Like what?" I asked, never before having given much thought to the subject, though it was intriguing me now.

"Maybe, we could go faster than the speed of light . . . something that must happen if we're ever going to space travel outside of our galaxy."

My brain whirling, "What about time travel?"

"Good," Max's enthusiasm infected the conversation. "How about telekinesis, and telepathy?"

"Wow," I said, then added, "maybe we could learn to heal ourselves."

"And have unlimited energy, maybe through cold fusion," he added.

We batted around more ideas for the rest of the afternoon.

As darkness approached, we gathered our trash and deposited it in the bins. On the walk back to my car, Max inquired, "Do you need to go right home?"

I thought of the tension and discomfort between my wife and me, so I said, "Not really. What do you have in mind?'"

"It'll be a surprise. You drive. Head north on Downing."

I followed Max's directions.

"Turn left here," Max pointed as we reached Nineteenth Avenue.

We had come to a large, dull-colored hospital building.

"But this is Children's Hospital," I exclaimed.

"Yeah, I know. Follow me inside. I want to show you something."

I never liked hospitals, especially ones for children, but curiously followed Max in.

"We're going to the oncology ward," Max volunteered.

I gulped. Dying children hurt the most. Jenny and I were never able to have children, and that former sadness jarred me like a punch.

We checked in at the nurse's station. You would have thought Max knew everyone. One of the nurses turned on the speaker, "Everyone, we have a special visitor on the floor. Max will tell stories in the TV room."

Squeals of laughter pealed throughout. Max and I were soon surrounded by throngs of children, each giggling, "Tell us a story. Tell us a story."

Kids everywhere, they seemed to range in age from six or seven up to eleven or twelve. With two sitting on his lap, others spilling over on chairs and on the floor, Max waited until it got quiet, after the many "shhs" from the older ones.

I looked around as children were being wheeled in on beds or wheel chairs, IVs following alongside, and felt as uncomfortable as I've ever been. You could tell the different stages the children were in: some had most of their hair; some just patches; a few were completely bald.

As Max began, I kept noticing out of the corner of my eye one little girl, as bald as an egg, staring at me.

I'm sure my body language and facial expression openly declared my discomfort, for when Max finished with the first story the little girl whose eyes I had been evading walked over and whispered, "Hey mister, you don't have to be afraid."

Her candor embarrassed me, but I was able to get out, "What's your name?"

She smiled and said, "Angela. What's yours?"

"Ross," I barely whispered.

With great earnestness she stated, "You know, everyone's going to die."

I stiffly nodded.

Then she sighed real big and spoke these haunting words I'll never forget. "I think I have it figured out," she continued. "See we're all given assignments here on earth . . . some of us are given longer assignments, and some of us have shorter ones . . . mine's just shorter," she said matter-of-factly and smiled up at me with the most beautiful brown eyes. I thought how close the name Angela was to "*angel.*"

My eyes filled with tears as I heard the deep wisdom her illness had somehow communicated to her. Turning to Max for help, I saw his own smile and tears cascading down his face.

The next thing I knew Angela had crawled into my lap. "Thanks for coming," she whispered. "If it's okay I'd like to just sit on your lap and listen to Max's next story."

I felt her thin but warm arm encircle my neck and her fresh-from-a-bath smell rising from her like an aura. She and I listened to Max's next story.

Finishing, he was greeted with loud clapping; then the kids were herded back into their rooms.

Angela had held on to me the whole time, all the while my almost forgotten feelings for fatherhood ran rampant. Before arising she kissed me on the cheek. "I really hope you'll come back."

With a lump in my throat that felt the size of a watermelon, I barely eked out that I would and solemnly followed Max back to the car.

Getting in, I stayed tongue-tied. Max was the one who broke the ice. "I know at first it's hard to go there, but once you're in . . . every time I get something most worthwhile."

I nodded feebly and started the car. Two men: one old, one young. Two friends, who had just learned some incredible wisdom from a small, dying eleven-year-old.

Before getting out of the car, Max spoke softly, like at the beginning of our day. "Remember earlier when I said how our attitude affects everything?"

"Yes," I answered.

"Well, let me tell you another story.

"Two complete strangers met on a path in the woods. Going to the same destination, they decided to travel together. One man believed the path led to a great, wondrous city; the other to no place special. Neither knew what they were going to find.

"During their journey they encountered both difficulties and good times. All the while one perceived it as an almost holy expedition. He saw obstacles as tests of his commitment, pleasant surprises as blessings of encouragement. The other believed none of this and experienced the whole trip as nothing more than a difficult, meaningless journey.

"When they arrived at their destination, do you know what happened?" queried Max.

Feeling a twinge of déjà vu, I shrugged.

Max gave me a smile, looking at me with enigmatic eyes. "They were both right!" he said, and with that was out of the car and gone.

Max's smile was contagious, and mine lingered on my face long after he was gone. I put the car in gear and made my way back home. I pondered his story. It haunted me, though I didn't know why at the time.

Arriving home, I was actually glad Jenny was still up. In what seemed an off-handed attempt to be nonchalant she inquired, "Why so late?"

We had been communicating so sparsely, either verbally or physically, the tension was thick.

"You remember I was having lunch with Max—that fellow I met at the bar?"

"Yeah, I just thought you'd be home sooner," she retorted.

Taking a deep breath, I began. "Look, can I share something really important that just happened to me?"

She froze, and the air turned to icicles.

Understanding she might be misinterpreting what I was about to say—maybe she thought I was having an affair, or wanted a divorce—I quickly relayed the trip to Children's Hospital and the amazing truth little Angela had shared with us.

Jenny's eyes softened for a moment, then filled with tears. Arising from the chair she quietly said, "That's really nice," then walked out of the kitchen.

I stood up and reached for her. "Jenn."

She stopped as I approached. Slowly encircling her with my arms, I awaited the normal stiffening, but it never occurred.

Not knowing what to say, I laid my chin upon her head and held her until both our sobbing subsided. When I let go, she continued her journey out of the kitchen and away from me.

The greatest discovery
of our generation
is that human beings
can alter their lives
by altering their
attitudes of mind.

— William James

CHAPTER TWO
Commitment

JUNE 8, 1998

I remembered her words so well.

"You know you might spend a little more time with me . . . and don't give me that lame excuse about working hard so we can have more . . . Ross, we already have more than most people in the world could dream of having . . . what is wrong with you?" She broke down sobbing. "What is wrong with us?"

I went to her. Tried to hold and console her. After only seconds, she shook her head and walked away.

She was right. There was something wrong with us. I just didn't know what to do, or . . . maybe . . . just didn't care enough anymore.

✳   ✳   ✳

JUNE 28, 1998

I don't know where Max got money to live on. He rented half of an older brick duplex in the Capitol Hill area of Denver, where trees had matured grandly and old red bricks aged like wine. A modest home on the outside, the inside was like a library, the number of books phenomenal. If pictures on walls are supposed to disclose our hidden selves, who we are, Max's disclosed nothing, for there was simply no room. Thousands of books, all sizes and colors, on every conceivable subject, lined every square inch of wall space.

Browsing randomly I chose one. Sensing Max behind me, I teasingly asked over my shoulder, "You haven't really read all of these books?"

"You bet. Some twice. Which one do you have there?"

"Something on commitment," I said, looking down at the worn cover.

"Take it with you," he encouraged, "but let's go. I'm starving and anxious to meet your wife."

After settling in the car, I poked fun again. "Max, no one's ever read that many books. Maybe we can get you in the *Guinness Book of World Records*?"

He laughed, and then volunteered, "I had to catch up. See I quit school after the eighth grade, or maybe they asked me to leave, I can't remember." A bittersweet smile crossed his face. "I was too smart for my britches. School appealed to me like the flu."

"You mean you started reading after you quit school?"

"Oh, no. Books didn't come till way later. It took me a long while to realize I wasn't as smart as I thought . . . so actually, I had to go back and learn. I was thirty-two before I could read well."

"Jesus," I said, "it seems you've caught up."

He smiled appreciatively.

No doubt Max and I were getting close, yet part of him he kept hidden, disclosing only a little at a time. Kind of like peeling an onion, I thought to myself. He continued to surprise me, with his depth as well as his faults. Maybe this is what relationships are all about: slowly unfolding, masks removed only gradually, all in the context of safety. The idea's newness vibrated deep inside me.

My home life didn't teach me much about how people interacted. Thinking it peculiar to be learning about relationships from a man—another male—I shifted my thoughts to Jenny, my wife, and the difficulties we were having just as Max and I arrived home.

Their connection was immediate. Genuine, gentle and charming, Max softly enfolded her hand as I introduced them, all the while studying her face intently. She of course blushed, pinkness spreading across her throat, a reaction I knew well. Sensing her discomfort, Max quickly put her at ease by complimenting her hair, a feature she secretly prized. How did he know? From then on they laughed and flirted, teasing non-stop, each enjoying the other immensely.

I hadn't mentioned that Jenny and I were having serious problems, though Max must have seen it. He also must have seen that I was losing her. He never commented, only shared a story on our drive back to his home at the end of the evening.

"I sure liked your wife."

"No kidding," I retorted. "I was almost jealous watching you two flirt."

He smiled, and then paused.

"I heard a story one of the big college football coaches told; I forget which one. Anyway, this coach was giving a talk on commitment, how important it was to be committed to whatever you're doing in life: football, business, school, home life, anything.

"He shared something about himself and his wife. 'Being committed to football was easy,' he said, 'but that wasn't so with my wife!' He said he'd gotten married right after college because it seemed like the thing to do—everybody else was. But he confessed that he had never committed to her. So obviously their marriage began having problems. Lots of problems. After a while he began to think he didn't love her any more, or doubt if he ever even had; so he began to speculate on how to get out of it.

"Then one day, for whatever reason, he realized something important. He realized he was good at football because he was committed to it. He then somehow bridged this thought to the relationship with his wife and realized his problem. The coach said it was a turning point in his life. Right then, for the first time, he committed himself wholeheartedly to her.

"'And you know what?' the coach wrote, 'A surprising thing happened. Suddenly my wife became more beautiful than I remembered, more sweet and loving. Today I am the luckiest man in the world for having been married to this wonderful woman for thirty-five years.'

"He confessed he still didn't know how his committing changed everything; all he knew is that it worked and turned out to be the best thing he had ever done."

Silence followed Max's story. No reference was ever made to Jenny and me.

After dropping Max off, I drove around for hours mulling thoughts over. I'd always believed the act of marriage itself was the commitment, never guessing real commitment required more—more frequency, more genuineness, more tenacity.

Jenny and I had been married twenty years, and I will be damned if I know when the spark went out. Knowing so little about healthy relationships, I guess I presumed the initial spark would just stay forever.

We married just out of college like most did, thinking it was the next logical step. Neither Jenny nor I could ever have been described as great looking. But I loved her dark, auburn hair, thick and luxurious. It swayed so beautifully when she talked, her head movements always accenting the important. She had a good figure then, and still does. But one day I looked up at her and suddenly realized somewhere along the way our relationship had become stagnant.

Don't get me wrong, our marriage wasn't bad. We had just become more like roommates, two separate people sharing the same home.

Questions ran through my mind often: When did the spark die? How did it die? And does it happen in all marriages?

Having no other males to discuss it with, I had struggled with how to get it back, but no solutions surfaced . . . until Max's talk on commitment.

That night I decided to try the coach's advice and commit. My expectations weren't very high; I just hoped she and I could get out of our rut, maybe even recapture a little of what we'd lost. Little did I know the startling effect it would have.

※　※　※

We started off with talks—long talks with one another.

Both of us, of course, were hesitant to be the first to say anything vulnerable. You might describe our conversations as even mundane, though for us it was a beginning.

After a while, our talking took on new meaning. We began to open up a little and share—our deepest yearnings, our failures, or earlier dreams which now would never be met, and our hopes for the future.

Somewhere along the way, we decided we needed to set aside one special night a week. We called it our date night—Friday was elected.

We had tried making love again, but it was dispirited, unpassionate for both of us. So I began searching the library for books on how to recapture the old flame. In one of the magazines I read was an interview with the actor Sean Penn. The interviewer asked many questions, but the one that stood out went something like this:

"Well, now that you're married, do you ever miss having a glamorous and different woman every night?"

I loved his response. First he stared at the interviewer for a moment, the article said, then he leaned forward and with great intensity said, "I'll tell you what is great, and it's not going to bed every night with a different women. What is great is going home and making love with the same woman every night."

Jenny and I were lying in bed after one of our Friday night dates, going through our routine of foreplay, neither of us really into it, when I stopped and began searching

Jenny's face, exploring every inch, something I hadn't done in a long while. When she asked what was wrong, I smiled then repeated the interview with Sean Penn.

I explained to Jenny that after reading it I realized how lucky I was having her . . . that with our history, both ups and downs, that I have just begun to see her as a rare and fine wine.

Telling her this, I watched as her eyes filled with tears, and then she released more passion on me than ever before.

So, as I said, "Little did I know the startling effect Max's story would have on our relationship!"

CHAPTER THREE
Life Philosophies

JULY 6, 1998

I picked up Max at his home. I'd been whining to him over the telephone how one of my investments had gone south, losing money, and I was berating myself unmercifully.

Getting into the car, he handed me three books: *Illusions* by Richard Bach, *The Prophet* by Kahlil Gibran and *Einstein's Dreams* by Alan Lightman. "Read these. They might help you out with the situation you're in." Indifferently tossing the books into the back seat, I started up again feeling sorry for myself.

"Max," I whined, "it isn't fair. I researched the deal thoroughly. I thought I structured it well. And it looked as if my downside risks were minimal . . . then everything went to hell. It just isn't fair."

"Life isn't fair," Max wholeheartedly agreed.

Surprised at his agreement rather than his usual challenges, I extended my whining. "No it isn't. I know it . . . I mean, I'm an adult and all . . . but damn it, this one should have been safe, and only the oddest, most unexpected event killed it—the original survey of the land proved incorrect . . . I feel like such a loser!"

"Sometimes things happen which at first seem lousy, but later prove to be good," he inserted.

"Oh, come off it, Max, you're not going to give me that 'when life gives you lemons, make lemonade' crap are you? That positive attitude junk does not make me feel better." And I continued ranting on and on.

Max listened sympathetically until I'd finished, then challenged me with this:

"You know, I heard about an American Indian who lived in Montana, I think it was. His tribe was small, very poor. Well, one day his horse, one of the few owned in the village, ran away and was captured by a bigger tribe living on the other side of the mountain range.

"Well, horses were very, very important in his little village, so everyone came to console him. Interestingly though, his father, who was chief, did not console him. Instead he posed his son a question: 'What makes you so sure this isn't a blessing?'

"Some months later, guess what happened? Not only did his horse return, but also brought with her a splendid pure-black stallion. This time the villagers gathered around to congratulate him—everyone except the father, who challenged him by asking, 'What makes you so sure this isn't a disaster?'

"No doubt their household was richer because of the two horses, especially with the addition of the fine stallion, which the son loved to ride. But one day he fell off the horse and badly broke his hip. Everyone in the village now came to console him. Once again though the father asked, 'What makes you so sure this isn't a blessing?'

"A year later their enemies came across the mountain, raided their village and forced every man and boy who could fight to go into battle with them. When it was over, almost all the males from the village had lost their lives. Only because the son was lame did he and his father survive to take care of each other."

I felt the silence between Max and me. But still being so negative and self-pitying, I growled, "Okay, what's the meaning of that?"

Max looked me square in the eyes, arms crossed and sadly shook his head.

It's a funny thing. I knew he knew that I really understood the meaning of the story. And he knew I wasn't in the mood for any idealistic crap. Yet inside my heart, despite my contrary mindset, I already sensed the truth. I learned from it, and from the fallout of that bad investment, because of its failure, I found a way to not only recapture the loss but also make even more money.

What I did was go back and pay for a new survey. None of the other people involved went along with me. "Why put more money into a bad deal," they said. "We're out of this one. You do whatever you want."

So I was the only one left, and would have to bear all the additional expenses myself. But, I kept remembering Max's story. Maybe some of the things that seemed bad at the time were actually . . . blessings in disguise.

Paying heavily for a fast, but much more comprehensive survey, I discovered a gem. The new survey not only expanded the amount of land I would actually be buying, but also included a small commercial piece that proved especially valuable.

✻　✻　✻

Max had a story for every situation. Never preaching, seldom even giving a clear answer, his tales helped me perceive situations differently, allowed me to arrive at my own solution. Only now, looking back, can I truly appreciate his wisdom and unique way of giving.

Like the time after I'd become wealthy, yet was bitching and moaning about how much extra stress the wealth brought. Instead of mocking me, Max nodded agreement, affirming my poor, poor predicament, then began the telling.

"Did you hear about the guy walking in the woods?" Max began, smiling mischievously.

I played along. "No, but I'm sure I'm going to."

Without missing a beat, he proceeded.

"Well, while out walking one day he came upon a ferocious grizzly bear which began chasing him. The man ran as fast as he could until he had to halt abruptly at the edge of a steep cliff. Seeing no other option, he decided to jump into the canyon below. Fortunately, at the last instant, he noticed a vine at the cliff's edge just long enough to reach the canyon floor below. Quickly scampering over, he cautiously climbed down the vine. After going a ways he looked down, only to see another ferocious grizzly bear awaiting him at the bottom. While pondering his dire predicament, he noticed above him and slightly out of reach two mice nibbling away on his vine. Frantic, he searched for another escape. To his surprise he discovered a small strawberry patch growing vertically out of the cliff, one plant heavily laden with the biggest, reddest, most beautiful strawberries he'd ever seen. So he plucked one, ate it and found it was the best strawberry he'd ever had."

Finishing, Max added nothing, just sat there smugly in silence.

Deep inside me, the answer rattled around on the fringe of my consciousness, but never revealed itself, nor did I see any connection of the story to my current state. Finally not able to contain my lack of patience any longer, I lost the stare down. "Okay, what does it mean?"

Max grinned, not pompously, but certainly with satisfaction.

"The moral of the story is this: There will always be a bear behind you and a bear in front of you, and usually there will be mice chewing on your lifeline. But in spite of that, if you can still find and enjoy the strawberries in life, you will have truly lived."

This message took time to register, but I finally saw it. To learn to enjoy life even in the midst of all the crises and difficult times was a completely new concept for me. Since I had begun to find myself in more and more tough spots as my investments expanded, I usually stayed mostly uptight— at the office, with Jenny, with friends.

I cut out a picture of some strawberries from a magazine and now carry it around in my wallet. Anytime I sense my stress level getting out of hand, I have learned to take out the picture, which always reminds me that now is the time to enjoy myself—even in the midst of challenges.

The results proved stupendous: My Mylanta usage decreased drastically, and the people who worked for me began saying how much more relaxed I seemed (probably meaning I was nicer to be around).

But the effect on my relationship with Jenny proved the greatest. We certainly became much closer after I had recommitted myself to her. Yet now things were even better. Every once in a while I'd catch Jenny staring at me when she thought I wouldn't notice. It made me uncomfortable until she followed with a kiss on my cheek, a small confident grin playing across her face.

After our next Friday night date, we were cuddling in bed when I shared my newest rekindle-your-sex-life find.

Whispering in Jenny's ear, I told her I had the unusual thought that even though we had been together a long time, that each day, each minute, each second our cells were constantly changing and being renewed. Therefore, I further explained, each time we made love, in a sense, I was actually making love to a brand new woman, one who was both different and better than before.

Her response matched her earlier one. There was no doubt I had to keep finding these little, new ideas. I just wondered if I'd be able to keep up with my wife.

Later that evening and after Jenny had fallen into a well-deserved sleep, I returned to my reading of *Illusions* by Richard Bach, one of the books Max had loaned me.

CHAPTER FOUR
Believing in God

AUGUST 4, 1998

"Hey Max, you believe in God?" We were hiking in an isolated, beautiful area near Deckers, southwest of Denver. Though Max was older, I was breathing harder.

"That's a deep one," he responded. Watching him mull it over, I waited.

"Yeah I do." He looked in my eyes, his as clear and pure as the sky above us. "Only I don't know how and can't explain why."

I nodded a silent understanding.

"There was this great philosopher named Immanual Kant," Max said, "known for a lot of things, but perhaps best known for refuting the logic proving God existed. In that day, see, there were three accepted theories: the

---

teleological, ontological and another I've forgotten. Everyone at that time agreed these theories logically proved the existence of God. Everyone that is, except Kant, who shocked the world by refuting them, by demonstrating it was impossible to prove God existed through logic. What's neat is I read somewhere that after finishing his paper, Kant turned it over to his editor and publisher, went home to his study, got down on his knees and prayed!"

I smiled, surprised. Max grinned.

"I like that story," he affirmed. "It's kind of the way I feel. Maybe you can't prove it logically, but still somehow you know He exists."

We sat there lost in our thoughts until something from long ago eased into my memory. "Hey Max," I spoke up, "this may be hard to believe but I have a story."

Eyes appreciative, he gave his full attention.

"One day an African tribesman was sitting on a rock by a stream, eating a mango, while looking down into the water. Suddenly, like a lightning bolt he instantly understood the meaning of life, the glory of creation. He realized we are all born of God and for the first time saw the perfection of God's plan for the universe, and a sense of peace spread over him.

"Quickly he ran back to his village to share his overwhelming experience. Crowds gathered around him, everyone in awe, all wanting to have his same experience.

Questioning him again they called out, 'And how did you find this wonderful knowledge that makes your face be filled with such light?'

"'I'm not sure,' the tribesman admitted. 'All I know is that this morning I was sitting on a big rock down at the stream below our village, eating a mango, gazing into the water, when all of a sudden truth revealed itself to me.'

"Upon waking the next morning, the enlightened tribesman found his village empty. Puzzled, he searched everywhere but could find no one. Finally giving up, he decided he'd think more upon his dilemma at his favorite spot down at the stream. Upon arriving, he surprisingly found the whole tribe, all huddled together on the big rock, all eating mangoes—all staring into the water.

"Do you get it?"

Max's face was blank until finally nodding, "Yeah. I think it means each of us can only find God through our own experience, not through someone else's."

"Max," I lauded, "you're brilliant!"

He liked that.

Our eyes drifted back to the beauty surrounding us, somehow more aware, more appreciative of these incredible Colorado Rocky Mountains.

And if you would know God be not therefore a solver of riddles. Rather look about you and you shall see Him playing with your children.

And look into space; you shall see Him walking in the cloud, outstretching his arms in the lightning and descending in the rain.

—Kahlil Gibran

The Prophet

CHAPTER FIVE
The Healing

AUGUST 22, 1998

We were driving east on Sixth Avenue toward the former Lowry Air Force Base, now a huge housing development. As always it was difficult not to appreciate the towering stately trees lining the flowered center park strip separating the opposing boulevards. We had just turned right onto Pontiac Street when a frightened squirrel darted in front of my car. Not having time to stop or veer away, I felt the slight bump and presumed the wheel crushed the little animal.

"Quick! Stop!" Max directed me.

Even before the car completely halted, Max was out the door. Running back to where the squirrel lay, he bent down and gently picked up the still, furry animal. Stroking it softly, he murmured something inaudible. Seeing the large smear of blood on the pavement, I shook my head at the futility of his actions. I was about to inform him of this fact when suddenly the tail twitched. Then again. And again. In a blur the little creature jumped out of Max's hand and ran up the nearest tree, chattering the whole way.

"Well, I'll be damned!" Max said. "I guess we must have missed him after all," and returned to the car.

Me—well I had a lump in my throat and wore a look of complete disbelief. See, there really was too much blood reddening the street.

Entering the car, I tried to talk with Max, to ask him what had just happened. But he only stared out the side window, whistling some little tune, ignoring me.

That was the first time.

The Things
I Have Done,
ye can do even more.

—Jesus of Nazareth

CHAPTER SIX

Love

SEPTEMBER 16, 1998

On one hand, Max openly displayed his emotions, allowing me to feel comfortable showing mine. On the other, I sensed he limited this emotional catharsis solely to the arena of storytelling. All others he maintained as tightly packed as sardines. It was a nuance I originally missed, only later realized.

This holding back occurred in all areas except one— love. Here he lacked control, had no subtlety, no pretense. Here his emotions ran freely, like a raging river breaking through dikes and sandbags, like an infant's innocent crying, unashamed. Whenever Max spoke in this arena, his eyes became hollow, sad and a shift took place strong enough to alter a room's atmosphere. Speak of love and he might hide behind quotes or share a thought that had been patiently waiting on his tongue, sometimes emerging at appropriate places, others not. It was as if his mood swings were conditioned by some private hiding place within him.

He once told me about a man named Leo Buscaglia, a good teacher who became a great one after developing a college course on love. Max explained how he arrived at it.

"This Buscaglia fellow had been a teacher all his life, working his way up from high school to college. In one of his classes he befriended a student who never missed class. But one day he became aware he hadn't seen her for a while. Checking the attendance records, he found she'd been absent a full week. Bothered, he asked around campus until to his horror, he discovered she'd committed suicide!

"This was the catalyst for Buscaglia's teaching change," Max excitedly explained. "It altered his total ideology. He began to focus on imparting knowledge normal textbooks didn't deal with, namely love and living skills."

Thinking back, I wondered if the story reflected Max's own desires, to better understand loving and how to teach the skills for it. I too had heard of Leo Buscaglia, but hearing it then from Max caused me to question my own business practices. Had I been giving enough attention and caring to the people who worked for me? Was I looking at others only for what they could do for number one? Should

I stretch myself to become involved with employees' personal lives? Should I be more vulnerable with them, or would that make me seem weaker, less competent?

✳   ✳   ✳

As I've said, Max's collage of emotion during his stories made it easy to miss how restrained he kept himself other times. Like all great storytellers or actors, he maintained control to show just the right amount of emotions to attain the right effect.

I saw him completely lose it only once, where he broke down sobbing. We'd spent the afternoon together, having lunch and a movie. I forget the title, except it revolved around a young boy with a tragic family life. Max's mood dramatically shifted somewhere during the film and was later reflected in his subdued demeanor on the trip home. There was no conversation, just silence.

Arriving at his curb, I tried to think of something to say. Fortunately he spoke first, softly.

"I'm sorry for being so quiet," he said, then tried to switch the mood by asking, almost pleadingly, "We had a good afternoon though, didn't we?"

I nodded yes.

He still didn't get out, just sat there looking down at the floorboard, until at long last he spoke.

"There was a little girl in an orphanage who wasn't very big, nor attractive. Had come from a bad home." He was almost whispering. "See, being so unattractive, she'd developed some behavior problems that always got her into trouble, especially at the orphanage. These in turn caused the superintendent to watch her more closely, always hoping to catch her doing something bad and expel her. But like all of us," Max peered earnestly at me, "she wasn't anywhere near as bad as the superintendent thought.

"Well, one day another kid reported to the superintendent she'd seen the little girl writing notes to someone on the outside of the institution. Suspicious, the superintendent told the girl to come and tell her the next time it happened.

"It wasn't long before the child came running back, 'She's written another note and hid it in a tree near the wall.'

"The superintendent and an assistant ran out to intercept the note before anyone else might get it. However upon opening and reading it, the superintendent's eyes filled with tears, and she silently passed the note to her assistant.

"The assistant read it. It simply said, 'To whoever finds this, I love you.'"

Tears streamed down Max's cheeks while he spoke the last line, "To whoever finds this." His shoulders began shaking and deep, deep sobs erupted from this gentle man.

I scooted over to put my arm around his shoulder and hold him while he cried, half expecting him to shrug me off. But he didn't.

They say stories we remember mirror our subconscious. In retrospect, I believe Max shared something so deep that few others, if any, had been told something so vulnerable. I felt honored—and saddened.

✳ ✳ ✳

Another technique Max employed in diverting attention from his emotionalism included humor, like the time he quickly shifted to this little story after relating something sad.

"There was once this man really concerned about his wife's health. She'd lost her sparkle, moped around and had no energy whatsoever. He took her from doctor to doctor, and no one could find the problem.

"Eventually one doctor became strangely interested in the woman's condition. Staring at her for a long time, he finally walked over and kissed her on both cheeks.

"Well, the results were amazing. Color returned to her face. Her eyes regained their sparkle. Her energy came back.

"The doctor then turned to the man and said, 'I think she's well.'

"'But how?' the husband exclaimed. 'How did you do it?'

"'Easy,' explained the doctor. 'Your wife just needs to be kissed twice a week.'

"Exasperated, the man replied, 'I don't understand it, but you're the doctor. Is it all right if I bring her in on Tuesdays and Thursdays?'"

Of course, I laughed because it was funny, though there's much I wish I could ask Max now. But then it didn't seem appropriate, or perhaps I was too busy absorbing his little lessons.

I came across a quote the other day from the French philosopher Teilhard de Chardin. It reminded me of Max.

"Someday, after mastering the winds, the waves, the tides and gravity, we shall harness for God the energies of love, and then, for a second time in the history of the world, man will have discovered fire."

I ache to know if I'd shown Max enough.

Most people show more persistence in the first year of life than they do all the rest—otherwise they never would have learned to walk . . .

Tenacity is the key to success. Remember diamonds are chunks of coal that stuck to their job!
—Daniel Guggenheim

CHAPTER SEVEN
Persistence

As the gods continued smiling down, my wealth multiplied. Each day brought vast financial transactions that only a few years ago would have been intimidating. Some days I risked and won; fewer days I lost.

There were also days when my anxiety level soared off the scale, when all I craved was a stress-free solitude, when I wanted nothing less than to quit. At these times, Max's stories magically materialized.

"I heard about this kid who was a senior in high school and wanted to go to college. The problem was he'd goofed off his first three years and only became serious the final year. While his grades were excellent his senior year, his earlier poor grades kept his overall average low.

"But he was determined. Obtaining applications for five different colleges, he thoroughly filled out each one, included his high school transcripts, mailed the package off to each university and anxiously awaited their responses.

"It took eight weeks before he received the first non-acceptance. The second rejection followed shortly. Then the third and fourth. Finally, upon receiving the fifth college's response—'we are sorry to inform you we are unable to accept your application for our freshman class . . .'—something shifted inside him, and he became angry.

"Now what's interesting here," I remember Max adding, "is that instead of quitting and feeling sorry for himself, he immediately sat down and composed a letter to the last school which rejected him.

"'Dear Sirs,' he wrote, 'I have just received your letter of refusal to admit me into your school. After receiving four prior rejections, yours was the one that broke the camel's back. Therefore, I have decided to "reject" your rejection, and will report as scheduled to classes September 2.'

"Well," Max added with indignation, "the admission person's first response was shock, then admiration, and she took it to the committee. Never having had an applicant reject their rejection, they eventually reversed themselves and allowed him to begin." Max chuckled. "That kid enrolled in September and graduated with honors five years later!"

I don't know about anyone else, but quitting was an issue I struggled with whenever things became difficult. It seemed that when I didn't know what to do, I would leave—quit—try something else. I never knew, or couldn't sense, when it was best to take your losses or dig in deeper. As a teenager in gym classes, the teacher would usually write on my report card that I was the epitome of the phrase: "No guts, no glory." At the time I tried convincing myself it was only foolish games, that they really didn't mean anything in the long run, all the while secretly knowing I was a quitter. I was gutless.

To this day, when those old feelings return, I recall this story from Max:

"A struggling young artist in Kansas City wanted very much to make a living drawing cartoons. He applied to what seemed like every newspaper in the country only to be turned down, each one informing him he had no talent.

"Depressed, broke, he found himself living in a dilapidated, mouse-infested garage with no future prospects. But he didn't quit. Instead, having only time on his hands, he made sketches of the garage and the little mice in it. Since they were his only company, he soon became intrigued with the little guys, especially one with whom he developed a friendship."

I can still visualize Max's expression forming for the surprise punch.

"This man didn't know at the time just how important his friendship with that one little mouse would become.

"See," Max burst out, "the man's name was Walt . . . Walt Disney, and the mouse became Mickey, and you know what happened after that."

* * *

On another occasion when I again flirted with dissolving my business interests, Max, after acknowledging the possibility it might be a good time to cash out, shared this little story.

"Back in 1904, a husband and wife scraped together all their money to purchase a booth at the St. Louis world fair. They risked everything.

"Things went well at first. They sold loads of waffles, that is until running out of paper plates and learning they couldn't get more." Max reminded me, "Remember, things weren't as available then as they are now, and not being able to obtain plates for the butter and syrupy waffles meant financial doom. It was not something they'd anticipated.

"Depressed. Angry. They were just about ready to give up when one of them had an idea. Racing home from the fairgrounds, they worked all night with their waffle batter making thousands. Only this time they did something quite different. This time they ironed them flat, then rolled them up into circular cones. First thing the next morning they located some ice cream," Max's face was aglow, "and for the first time in the history of the United States placed a scoop of ice cream on each waffle and served the world's first ice cream cones.

"They made a fortune," Max laughed, "by not giving up."

The last story especially helped to remind me of the importance of not giving up in my relationship with Jenny.

Looking back, it would have been so easy to have just walked away.

Instead, by not quitting, by consciously taking the risk of moving into unknown territory, we had discovered greater love.

*Nothing in the world can take
the place of persistence.
Talent will not; nothing is more common
than unsuccessful men with talent.
Genius will not; unrewarded genius
is almost a proverb.
Education will not; the world is
full of educated derelicts.
Persistence and Determination
are omnipotent.*

—Calvin Coolidge

CHAPTER EIGHT
Perception

OCTOBER 12, 1998

"Everything is perception."

"I thought you said everything was attitude," I challenged. We had just finished lunch and were just driving around some old residential parts of Denver.

"Well, attitude certainly affects how we perceive things, but perception is a major part of it all." We were both off a little today, slightly withdrawn.

"But if everything is perception," I pressed, "then what is reality? Is there even a true reality? Are there only atoms, or energy, or whatever we're made of just floating randomly around?"

Max shrugged. "Got me. Every time I think I know something, life knocks me for a loop." We laughed.

"Take four people standing on a street corner, all observing the same accident. Hell," Max emphasized, "any good attorney knows there's never just the one accident—each of those people will see something different.

"So," he asked, "who's right?"

I thought. "Okay, I agree that four people will each perceive the accident differently, but isn't there somewhere, some time, a place where only one accident occurs?"

I observed his brow furrow, eyes become intense, upper teeth gnawing on lower lip; then his face suddenly relaxed.

"There's an odd story I once read; I think it was about a couple of Hindu fellows, one a teacher—a really smart yogi—and the other a student. They were out in this field, the teacher standing, the student sitting on the ground, leaning against a tree. The student confessed one of the biggest obstacles to his growth was a desire to experience having a wife and children.

"His teacher looked upon his young, brilliant student and, rather than urging him to lose this dream, instead told him to close his eyes and concentrate on feeling the sun's relaxing rays shine upon his face. It was a beautiful day, and the sun's warmth spread across his body bringing drowsiness, until he soon fell asleep, his teacher standing before him.

"Suddenly the young man jolted awake to the sound of thunder and rain pouring down upon him. Jumping up, he looked for his teacher, but instead saw a great flood bearing down upon him. Unable to do anything, the young man was swept up in a wild, powerful flood that carried him away for a long, long time.

"Constantly struggling to keep his head above the water, he eventually saw a house with people standing on the roof. Swimming toward the roof, he held out an arm in hopes they could grab him. As fate had it, the man did just that, grabbed his arm and pulled him up out of the flood's dangerous current. Catching his breath, the young man thanked the older man who'd saved him and then noticed there were also an older woman and a beautiful young girl, probably, he thought, their daughter.

"After the flood receded, the older man invited the younger man to stay with them. He told him they could feed him and give him a room if he would help them clean up. Having nothing better to do, he agreed.

"As it happened they all soon became friends, weeks turned into months, and the boy helped with planting the crops and became indispensable with the other farm chores. He and the daughter also grew very fond of one another until a marriage was agreed upon.

"Life was good for them all; the young couple produced two wonderful children, a girl and boy. Eventually the parents passed on; the couple inherited the farm and became even more prosperous. The man achieved everything he wanted: a wife, children, farm, property, happiness, everything.

"Until one day a torrential rain came suddenly, followed by a huge flood. The man quickly ran to save his children, only to arrive just as the floodwaters sucked them under.

"Looking next for his wife, he saw the flood take her. Destroyed, grieved beyond all hope, he fell to the ground in anguish and was also swept away by the flood.

"The next thing the young man realized upon opening his eyes was the astonishing fact he was sitting in the original field, leaning against the same tree as before, his face warmed by the sun, his teacher standing before him smiling.

"Bewildered and confused, he pleaded for an explanation.

"Mischievously his teacher challenged, 'Now you tell me. Which experience is more real: the dream you just had, or the reality of us talking in this field?'

"Perplexed, the young man had no answer."

Eventually I looked over, a smile forming, "That Hindu student and yogi teacher, they're kind of like us, aren't they?"

Max grinned, "Maybe a little . . . but you're a lot smarter than the student, and I'm a lot dumber than the teacher," he said, his smile increasing.

I wasn't so sure.

*Suppose time is a circle, bending back
on itself. The world repeats itself,
precisely, endlessly . . .*
—Alan Lightman
Einstein's Dreams

CHAPTER NINE
Fatherhood

NOVEMBER 5, 1998

Arriving to pick him up, I was waved inside by Max. Entering, I was again taken back at the volume of books lining every wall, floor to ceiling.

He came in from the back carrying a photograph, holding it carefully. Sitting down close, he handed it to me.

"This is my son," he whispered.

"Your son," I exclaimed, taken aback.

He nodded. "I had a wife too, but we divorced a long time ago. I was a hothead, wasn't a good husband, even worse father . . . didn't see the boy for years. When I finally came to my senses as to what I'd done, I searched all over until I found him."

The ensuing silence was broken by his shaking voice, "He was grown, running with a tough crowd, mad at the world, hated me, said he'd gotten along just fine without me . . . I guess I'd screwed him up pretty bad."

"Wow," I said numbly. "Where is he now?"

"During one of my visits to try to get to know him, you know, reconnect and all, he died in a motorcycle accident, probably to spite me."

I didn't know what to say, so I grimaced, then asked, "Your wife?"

"Oh she died of cancer a long time go. So the boy didn't have anybody. By the time I found him, he was too far gone . . . alcohol, drugs, the people he ran with. It kind of confirmed I wasn't cut out to be a father, so I never remarried, didn't want to screw up anybody else."

Flabbergasted, I couldn't believe this from the man who'd taught me so much. I didn't know what to say, until an idea formed. "Hey Max," I said softly, "I don't know how you were before; maybe you weren't a good father then, but I bet you'd be one now."

His voice broke. "Thanks Ross," he said. "I appreciate it coming from you."

My memory slipped back to an earlier time. "Jenny and I couldn't have children," I shared. "We tried and tried until some tests showed it'd be impossible . . . probably for the best. My life wasn't great growing up, so I imagine I wouldn't have been much good at fatherhood either."

I felt Max observing me, then heard him say, "Maybe you wouldn't have then, but I bet you'd be now."

Sheepishly I smiled at his return favor, "Thanks."

We sat in his small living room filled with books while the sun filtered in through the window creating a surrealistic aura. Max held his son's picture across his chest, eyes far off to a world that was better; I recalled Jenny's overwhelming loss in not being able to have kids and was surprised to feel wetness on my own cheeks.

I stayed with Max all that afternoon, sitting in the quiet, hearing each other's breathing, and occasional soft crying. Max spoke only once. It sounded like a quote from the Bible, maybe Old Testament. "O my son. Absalom, my son, my son Absalom! Would I had died instead of you, O Absalom, my son, my son!"

CHAPTER TEN
The Second Healing

The next "incident" with Max proved even more powerful and confusing than the first.

We had been out hiking and came upon a fawn entangled in barbed wire. At seeing us it made another feeble effort to free itself, but the effort lasted only briefly as the poor thing was exhausted.

Approaching slowly, Max knelt down to help. I knelt beside him.

What I saw sickened me with despair. The struggling animal had pulled so hard its one leg was almost completely severed by the wire. The other leg had broken and jutted out at a peculiar angle. The poor young deer whimpered softly.

After untangling the wire, Max gently grasped each of

the injured legs. I saw his eyes close and wondered if he was crying. When my eyes returned to the fawn's legs, I gasped—they were whole and undamaged!

Helping the deer to rise, Max patted it on its skinny rump to urge it to run off. It was then that a large doe stepped out of the woods and made a sound. The fawn ran to her, and then both bolted away.

I peered over at Max only to see his moist eyes shining vividly.

"What was that, Max?"

Shaking his head in wonderment he just said, "I don't know," his unconvincing words echoed. Nor would he look me in the eyes. "Let's go," he said sheepishly.

We returned in silence to the car. Once again, I didn't know what to say.

*   *   *

I had trouble sleeping that night.

Twice could not be a fluke, nor coincidence, nor luck.

I had started to discuss what I'd seen both times with Jenny, but for some unknown reason just couldn't. I don't know why. It felt as if I were breaking some confidence.

And discussing it with Max proved just as difficult. I wondered how long he had known of his gift and how many times he had used it.

He always ignored any questions concerning it and gave off feelings that seemed to say, "I don't want to talk about this."

I hadn't told him, but there seemed to be a vague lightness beginning to surround his head. The light shone brighter during his healing of the deer, but seemed always there.

He didn't look sick, and when asked how he felt always retorted, "Never better," in a huffy kind of way. Other than the healings, and the faint glow, he seemed normal.

I just never would have guessed anything like this could ever happen.

CHAPTER ELEVEN
Prejudice

JANUARY 19, 1999

Martin Luther King Day.

Little aware of it besides banks and government offices being closed, I felt it more an inconvenience. But Max called, said we were going to a parade. I protested. He overrode me with unchallengeable logic: "Nothing much you can get done anyway, most places are closed."

Reluctantly agreeing, I began another lesson: overcoming prejudice or, perhaps in my case, apathy.

I drove to the parade. Max talked. "Growing up, I never knew people with black skin were called anything but 'niggers,' and brown skinned were called 'spics' or 'wetbacks,' Asian people, 'slanty-eyed,' 'gooks,' or 'chinks,' Egyptians, 'sand niggers,' or 'camel jockeys.'"

His directness shocked me. Glancing over I saw his moistened eyes, head angled downward, visibly ashamed.

Collecting himself, "Somebody once said, I forget who, that if the Creator waved a magic wand and made everyone the same—and I mean exactly the same: same sex, same color eyes, same weight—humankind would still have devised some system of prejudice by noon of that same day."

He further added, "Did you know the man who conceived the idea of blood banks could neither give nor receive blood because he was black?"

"Oh, come on Max," I doubted, "is that really true?"

He avidly nodded.

"I believe, clear to the bone, we must fight prejudice with all our might, starting first with ourselves, or it's going to kill us. It's the worst disease of humankind."

He paused a long while before beginning this:

"I heard a story about a German Lutheran pastor named Martin Niemuller. He wrote a lot about Nazi war camps. Wasn't too popular with other Germans, but that didn't stop him," Max snickered. "See, he believed we have to keep talking and writing about the Holocaust or we might forget it. Listen to this poem he wrote." Max quoted from memory.

"In Germany, the Nazis first came
for the Communists,

and I didn't speak up
because I wasn't a Communist.
Then they came for the Jews,
but I didn't speak up
because I wasn't a Jew.
Then they came for the Trade Unionists,
but I didn't speak up
because I wasn't a Trade Unionist.
Then they came for me . . .
By that time there was no one left
to speak up for me."

We sat in silence after Max finished, both perhaps sharing in some of the blame for those who did nothing to stop the greatest horror in human history.

❋   ❋   ❋

I joined my first civil rights march that day, only thirty-plus years after the first one in Alabama. You might say I was a wee bit late.

But I marched. Held hands with Whites, African Americans, Gays, Latinos, Native Americans, Asians and Max. And I felt good; hopeful for our world. It was a feeling I hadn't experienced in a long while.

*Men hate each other
because they fear each other;
they fear each other
because they don't know each other;
they don't know each other
because they are separated
from each other.*
—Martin Luther King

CHAPTER TWELVE
Unity of Humankind

AM I MY BROTHER'S KEEPER?
— *Genesis 4:9*

Behind all of Max's voluminous stories and friendship lay a deeper philosophy, a guiding principle he'd probably even spoken though I hadn't heard. You see, Max believed we were all one. I don't think he ever considered the possibility of separation, that people were inherently different. He simply, and utterly, perceived all people originated from the same source, whatever you might name it.

He would quote John Donne from memory.

"No man is an island entire of itself; every man is a piece of the Continent, a part of the main . . . any man's death diminishes me, because I am involved in Mankind; And therefore never send to know for whom the bell tolls; it tolls for thee."

Or the time he told me about a book he'd read entitled *Black Like Me,* written by a white author named Griffith.

Max explained the book focused on the prejudice, pain and separation black-skinned people in our country experience. Coming from a middle-income white family, the author admitted he'd had little firsthand interaction with Negroes. So to learn, he did some rather radical things to change his external appearance: took pills to darken his skin pigment, dyed himself all over, shaved his head, wore brown-colored contact lenses, worked on a dialect and began living as a black person.

Intrigued, I remembered listening intently.

"Do you know what he discovered?" Max asked.

"It's something no one should ever forget. He discovered the hard way that when you get to know the unknown person, that is any person seemingly different—you will find we are all the same!"

This was another difficult concept for me to integrate. Internally I immediately sensed its validity. Externally, day-to-day, I couldn't grasp it.

I grew up white in Middle America. Though my family was not wealthy at all, we still lived with the sense we were superior to everyone else in the world. I remember traveling to Japan. Only eleven years old, I asked the uncomfortable question to my parents, "If we are so superior to these people, how come they can speak two or three languages while we only speak one?"

The question obviously shocked them, for a blank look crossed their faces. The subject immediately changed and though unspoken, a strong sense of inappropriateness richly lingered.

In my family, the concept of all of us being "one" would have been ridiculed mercilessly. I remember my grandmother "advancing" to become liberal when she began referring to blacks as "Nigrahs," versus the degrading "niggers." The description "Mexican" was always said with disdain, or substituted with "wetback."

But I began to apply this concept in my everyday interactions with everyone. And amazingly, the more I practiced it the more I came to believe . . . that we are all one.

*Human beings have a
kind of optical illusion.
We think ourselves separate
rather than part of the whole.*
—Albert Einstein

CHAPTER THIRTEEN
Story of Healing

I just read a book, *Stronger at Broken Places,* by a man named Max Cleland," Max spoke. "The guy lost both legs and an arm back in 1968 fighting in Vietnam—a really stupid, stupid war, you know . . . But anyway, as you could imagine, he had to come to grips with a lot of things if he was going to go on. Depression, even considered suicide, until he finally pulled out of it.

"Now this man with no legs and only one arm overcame these handicaps, worked hard and eventually was appointed head of the National Veterans Administration at the age of only thirty-four, the youngest ever. Later, he was sworn in as Secretary of State for Georgia, I think. Anyway, this guy wrote this book, and maybe it's applicable to you and me.

"What Cleland discovered was that after a broken bone heals, it actually becomes stronger than it was originally at the place where the break occurred. Likewise, he discovered that after body tissue heals from a deep wound, the scar tissue forming over the wound becomes stronger than the tissue was in the first place!"

"Wow!" I exclaimed. "I like that."

Pausing, Max leaned over to whisper, "Maybe that's the way it is with you and me! Maybe now we really could be good fathers, whereas before it wasn't possible."

I couldn't speak, tried to smile. Max's demeanor mirrored mine—something had caught in his throat, too.

*Two paths diverged
in the woods, and I—
I took the one less traveled by . . .*

—Robert Frost

CHAPTER FOURTEEN
Change

FEBRUARY 8, 1999

Max had the uncanny ability to read people, a kind of sixth sense in knowing which story he needed to tell. Perhaps I unconsciously conveyed something, maybe through a mood or facial expression, I don't know. Yet I do know for certain there were times he received no external clues. He just knew.

Like the day I was feeling old. It seemed everything involved the newest gadgets—the fastest cable connections, advanced modems, the newest business programs, downloading, hardware I'd never heard of, wristbands, tiny laptops, online connections. My partners were younger, talked a different language, and to make things worse seemed embarrassed over my inability to follow them, though I was the one supposedly leading the venture. I tried bluffing to sound knowledgeable, but I knew they knew, so gradually I pulled out of the deal.

Grumpy, feeling like a dinosaur in this new-age communication world, I handled my situation like an "adult" and drove to my old, familiar bar. Here things were predictable: gleaming mahogany, crystal clear glasses, martinis cold as ice. It was the same place I'd first met Max, and true to form, he already occupied a seat. Saying nothing, I pulled a stool next to his, nodded and ordered.

He didn't stare direct, more oblique, assessing me. When the martini arrived I took a large sip, sighed deeply, and said, "Hello Max."

He sort of grinned out of one corner of his mouth, looked down into his beer as if reading tea leaves, and began to speak.

"I once heard about these Japanese monkeys," he started in, no preamble or anything, "who lived on this uninhabited island. No human whatsoever except for the scientists observing them. The scientists were watching their normal daily activities when something unusual occurred.

"See, these monkeys liked to eat sweet potatoes that were dropped in the sand by the scientists. Whereas they loved the potatoes, they did not like the sand.

"Well, one day a monkey accidentally dropped or threw a sweet potato into the ocean, which of course washed the sand off. Pretty soon thereafter, it was observed by the scientists, this one little monkey taught it to the other monkeys on the island, and news spread fast.

"Then an amazing thing happened. At some point, when enough monkeys on this one island learned to wash off the sand in the ocean, let's say the hundredth monkey, an unexplainable phenomenon occurred. For some unknown reason, on the next island over, totally unconnected in any way to the first island, the monkeys there began doing the same thing!

"From a scientific viewpoint," Max inserted, "there was no logical reason. From a metaphysical viewpoint, a theory emerged." Like always Max knew how to pause for maximum effect. "At a point when a certain number of people grasp a new idea, say one hundred, the idea then somehow spreads or communicates to all other people on the same planet! Thus, the 'Hundredth Monkey Syndrome' sprang forth!"

I stared at Max in awe. Suddenly, I realized my mouth must have been ajar. Quickly swallowing and closing my mouth I exclaimed, "You've got to be kidding Max; that's the most amazing concept I've ever heard."

"Yep," he proudly nodded.

I continued gazing, still awed, in an almost reverential stupor, until he became uncomfortable and reminded me of my tendency to drool.

* * *

His next lesson on change was more personal, vulnerable. We, and I mean most people, aren't aware of how we come across to others, how they perceive us. Let me illustrate. I walked into the office of a title insurance company that handles all of my business. Before entering, for some reason I stopped, then before resuming, overheard at the doorway the conversation of two employees who were handling the closing. The main closer was talking to her assistant about me. What I heard was disturbing.

"Now, Mr. Jamison is a very important client to our company and is a nice person and all; but watch out, he's also a ruthless business man."

Stunned, but quickly regaining my composure, I entered smiling, went over the figures and signed everything needed, all the while pretending I'd heard nothing. Later, I confessed to Max my hurtful discovery, and that I didn't know how to change the tough facade I presented to others. His advice came in the form of a fairy tale, or at least I think it was.

"Once upon a time there was a hard-hearted king so unpopular he had to continuously fight off rebellions—even attempts on his own life. This continued until one morning he awoke and realized how miserable he was. More than anything else, he wished to change. Desperate, he called upon his royal wizard.

"After hearing the problem and pondering the situation, the wizard told the king, 'I can help you but you must be prepared to carry out any instructions I give you.'

"'Anything,' agreed the king, 'anything that will restore peace to me.'

"'Very well,' said the wizard, 'wait three days and I will bring you a gift.'

"When the days elapsed, the wizard brought the king a mask. It was almost an exact likeness of the king's face, yet had one very important difference: Instead of the usual frowns and scowling lines, this image was smiling and had smooth, pleasant features.

"'I can't wear that, the king argued, 'It's not my face, and besides, people won't recognize me. They know I'm not a happy man.'

"'If you want me to help,' the wizard reiterated, 'you must wear the mask at all times.'

"Begrudgingly the king agreed, and amazing things started happening. Instead of hating him, people began to actually like him, and felt more comfortable and safe around him.

"The king in turn responded positively to their acceptance and began treating them with kindness and respect. Soon the disobedience and unrest died down and peace was restored.

"Only one source of dissatisfaction remained for the king—within his own heart.

"Though greatly pleased with the new changes in his kingdom, he felt hypocritical because of the phony mask. He wrestled with his conscience until finally summoning the wizard.

"'I'm grateful to you for the changes that have taken place within the kingdom, but in my heart I feel I can deceive my subjects no more. Please allow me to remove the mask.'

"With a surprisingly auspicious look, the wizard agreed.

"Filled with shame, the king stood in front of a mirror and slowly peeled away the image of what had so transformed his kingdom and his own life. Fearful, but sensing it had to be done, he opened his eyes fully expecting to see his old scowling face.

"But surprisingly that's not what appeared. Instead, staring back from the mirror was a radiant, joyous face—only expressing even more happiness than the mask had. Realizing an inner transformation had occurred, the king saw that his face now reflected what his heart had become—

kind, generous and loving. He realized the mask had been only a temporary conduit, drawing out his true inner beauty."

I loved this little story, and from that day forward, each morning I practiced smiling in the mirror. I also paid attention to my facial expressions at closings and during negotiations, and especially around employees. It seemed rather tedious at first, but soon I became aware of how differently people responded. There was less tension, less contentiousness, more joviality. Almost miraculously my days became lighter. I made new friends, and gratifyingly, my business not only didn't suffer but also became more profitable.

CHAPTER FIFTEEN
A Parable on Death

SEPTEMBER 19, 1999

Late one morning, Max called at the office to twist my arm to go hiking. The aspen leaves had just turned that magical yellow-gold, the temperature low seventies, the sky an almost unnatural blue, the sun shining as clear and bright as it could. It was a crisp, exquisitely beautiful Colorado fall day. We drove to Georgetown, then followed the road up above town to Guanella Pass.

There are rare moments hiking this time of year when you suddenly walk into a grove of aspen and everything becomes too beautiful. The sun shimmers on the golden, yellow leaves, the wind is softly rustling, making them twinkle like diamonds, and you feel you've entered Camelot. Max and I had experienced this together a couple times before, each time believing it alone was the absolute best, every time grinning like idiots. Today was one of those.

On the hike back to the car Max's mood changed. Quiet and withdrawn, it was in contrast to our earlier deep connection. I allowed him his privacy.

Driving down the mountain, he broke the silence with this story, told very quietly, very solemnly.

"In a small body of water lived a colony of water bugs. Each generation lived like the other, always clinging to the muddy bottom, and forever gazing up through the murky waters at what seemed a source of light shining through. Every so often, one of them would accidentally lose his grip on the bottom and float up into the light, never to be seen again.

"While each generation forever pondered and debated the source of the light, as well as the fate of those who drifted up into it, one advanced generation decided to do something about it. Calling all the water bugs together, the ruling body of elders decided they would draw straws, the one with the longest would be the one to let go, float up toward the light, discover what it was, then return to share his findings with all the others on the bottom.

"The fateful drawing occurred, the longest straw holder agreed to the frightening task, made a solemn vow to return, let go, and immediately began the journey ascending up toward the light.

"Up, up, up he floated, scared to death, yet all the while transfixed as the light grew brighter and brighter. After a long while, the little bug finally reached the top only to discover he was in a small pond deep in the forest.

"Here he saw that the bright light turned out to be a magnificent yellow sun. And, though before everything had been filtered through the brown, murky waters, now he beheld everything clearly, in their rich, true colors. There were lush green grasses and trees, bright red and yellow flowers everywhere, and the sky that held the mesmerizing, golden sunlight was the most beautiful blue color imaginable.

"But just as he was experiencing these wondrous sights, a sudden tiredness came over him, causing him to go into a deep, deep sleep.

"Some time later he awoke, still on the pond, though now he noticed he'd grown wings, had turned into a dragonfly and could actually fly through the blue sky seeing even more beautiful sights. Flitting his wings, he soared and soared, never ceasing to be amazed, nor to appreciate his newfound freedom and paradise.

"Then suddenly he remembered his vow to return. Desperately, urgently, he had to tell them of the paradise above. So with a drop of his wings, he flew straight down into the water at a fast speed. Splat! He hit the hard surface, knocking himself out cold.

"Later upon awaking, he tried again, and again. Then twice more, each time knocking himself out longer. Finally, realizing he would be unable to return despite his promise, he now knew for certain each of the water bugs would have to find the truth himself.

"With that understanding, he flew off into the beautiful blue sky, with all the surrounding magnificent colors, basking in the bright yellow sunlight and lived happily for all eternity."

Max looked over at me. "I think that's what death is all about."

I loved his parable, told him so, but something kept me from taking it further, or asking why he'd even brought it up. His mood eventually changing for the better, he returned from his quietness, and we enjoyed each other's company on the drive home. He never mentioned it again. Nor did I.

What the caterpillar calls
the end of the world, the
Master calls a butterfly.

—Richard Bach

Illusions

CHAPTER SIXTEEN
A Death

Maxwell Winston Stone died November 4, 1999, exactly forty-six days from telling the water bug parable. I understand now why he shared it, but unaware of any illness, I'm perplexed how I'd intuitively sensed more, yet could or would not accept its deeper message. Like most, I'm only vaguely aware of something intangible within, a spark or light. But discussions with Max often ignited long forgotten self-realizations, and surprised me into remembering a part of myself long ago dimmed yet not extinguished: my soul.

He'd left a single envelope for me in his apartment. Emotions raced as I read the personal endearments. I eventually managed to comprehend the note's three requests.

Max was obviously embarrassed over lacking the funds to carry out his wishes, but knew I'd gratefully cover them.

First, he asked for a memorial service at Trinity United Methodist, a massive, old, ornate church in downtown Denver just off Broadway. Second, to be buried at Fairmount Cemetery on Alameda Avenue, one of the most beautiful anywhere, and oddly a place I'd frequented. Walking its grounds, awed by gorgeous giant trees, I would read and reread the most unusual, sometimes humorous tombstone inscriptions dating back from the mid-1850s, and peer curiously into large, expensive family crypts. I, too, had found serenity there—nothing morbid, just peace. The third and final wish was to place large obituary ads in Denver's two major newspapers, *The Rocky Mountain News* and *The Denver Post.*

* * *

The morning of his memorial service I had trouble getting out of bed: no energy, no strength, no will. Like a zombie in a trance, I absently went through motions as my nightmarish dreams crippled me with memories of my earliest loneliness. I had jolted awake twice. Sobbing out loud, being held tightly by Jenny each time until I drifted off, only to have the process repeat itself, my weakness clearly exposed as laundry hanging out to dry.

She drove. I couldn't. We claimed seats in the front pew reserved for family. Jenny was softly crying. I sat there feeling as lonely as a shipwrecked survivor on an uncharted, desert island and wondering whether being alive was a blessing or a curse. Although I was unsure I would be able to speak at all when the time came, the day before the service I had jotted down a few things to say about Max. We were expecting few, if any, attendees; so we were surprised at hearing the first rustlings behind us. The murmurings and sounds of footsteps, and of coats and purses being deposited on the pews grew louder and louder.

Finally turning around to see, I discovered a third of the huge church was occupied and more people were still arriving. By the time the service started, the church was filled to overflowing with people standing in the aisles and in the back. I never would have guessed that Max knew so many people. Jenny beamed openly and squeezed my hand so hard it hurt. I discovered a new supply of tears moistening my face.

Toward the end of the service, the minister asked if anyone wished to say anything about Max. Grasping the small piece of paper on which I had quickly scribbled my notes, I started to rise, only to freeze halfway up. A line was forming. I'd have to wait.

The first man to come forward looked like a street person, or maybe a former one: clothes old and too large, yet clean; long hair tied in a pony tail, washed; clean shaven; glasses mended by Scotch tape and string; shoes ancient and shined.

Intentionally holding his chin high, he began speaking haltingly, without confidence.

"Like maybe for some of you, life has been hard for me; it wasn't good growing up; bad afterwards, too." He looked down quickly, trying hard to control a quivering voice and emotionally charged body, then continued.

"The time I felt the lowest was when I met Max, or Maxwell W. Stone as he introduced himself. Me sitting in the gutter half-stoned, him leaning down to shake my hand. At first I thought he was making fun, me looking so pathetic and all. But he wasn't. He was different. Helping me walk to a restaurant where I wouldn't feel out of place, he fed me, then made me promise I'd meet him again tomorrow, same time. The next day turned into another, and a day after that, and the next. Max met me fourteen days in a row. The last six I was straight.

"On the fourteenth day he gave me a poem, one I'll never forget, never lose, because I keep it close and read it all the time." Pulling out a beat-up wallet, he extracted a well-used, often folded slip of paper.

"The poem's called, '*The Man in the Glass.*'"

"A lady named Ann Landers had it in one of her newspaper columns. She said it was mailed to her by a young woman whose brother was trying to get off drugs. They thought he was doing better but then he up and killed himself. This poem was found taped to the bathroom mirror." Hesitantly, filled with deep emotions, he recited:

"When you get what you want in your struggle for self,
and the world makes you king for a day,
Just go to a mirror and look at yourself,
And see what that man has to say.
For it isn't your father or mother or wife,
Whose judgment upon you must pass,
The fellow whose verdict counts most in your life,
Is the one staring back from the glass.
Some people might think you're a
straight-shootin' chum,
And call you a wonderful guy,
But the man in the glass says you're only a bum,
If you can't look him straight in the eye.
He's the fellow to please, never mind the rest,
For he's with you clear up to the end.
And you've passed your most dangerous, difficult test
If the guy in the glass is your friend.
You may fool the whole world
down the pathway of years,
And get pats on your back as you pass.
But the final reward will be heartaches and tears
If you've cheated the man in the glass."

Teary, lips quivering, he proudly faced us.

"Max helped me in a lot of ways since then, but the poem did the most. Somehow he knew I needed to hear it."

Silence enveloped the sanctuary as this gentle, hard-luck man finished talking. Head bent down in respect for Max, he began his journey to the back of the room until some people near the front waved him over to sit next to them. He surprisingly accepted, face moist, but no longer feeling separated. I later heard that someone offered him a job, one I understand he still has.

The next person to walk up was a stern-looking, middle-aged man accompanied by an older teenager, or perhaps young adult. Conservative and well dressed, the man's appearance contrasted sharply with the boy who had long hair and wore stylishly ragged, holey clothes. Turning to face the boy, his countenance melted and became glowing, love-filled. He began.

"I was brought up in a family where outward respect and appearance were the most important things. Not love. Not acceptance. Just outward appearances.

"I accidentally met Max at a bar recently after my son and I had a terrible fight, one where I'd thrown him out of the house, the house where he, my wife and I had lived his entire life, all seventeen years. It'd been two weeks since Robbie—I mean Rob," he quickly corrected himself, "had left. We heard no word on how he was doing, or even where he was staying, and I was torn between my stubbornness and concern.

"Well anyway, I was drinking heavily in this bar. A man casually sat down on the stool next to me. Mind you other stools were open. He could have chosen any of them, but instead chose that one. He didn't say much except 'Hello,' ordered a beer, and sat sipping quietly. I hadn't had anyone to talk with about my son's leaving, especially not my wife, who was totally crushed. I needed to talk about this, and ended up doing it with a complete stranger.

"I talked and talked. Max listened and listened, intently, until I'd finished. While I attempted to dry my tears with a tiny bar napkin, Max just politely stared down at his beer, though I surprisingly felt he'd connected with my pain. Then with no sense of judgment, no superiority, he told me a story.

"He said, 'I heard of quite a unique situation once. It was about a father who'd gotten into a fight with his son and told him to leave home, too. His son's name was Juan; they were from South America, I think.'

"Max told me the situation was like mine, although I think the son's absence was a bit longer. This father hadn't heard from his boy for maybe two or three months, when suddenly he broke down crying. Realizing his mistake, he frantically searched all over, everywhere, but no luck. As a last resort he had an idea: He would place an advertisement in the city's largest newspaper, a huge one that anyone reading couldn't possibly miss. The ad went something like this:

'Juan, my beloved son, forgive me. I love and miss you so. Please come back home. I'll meet you at 12:00 noon this Saturday at the city's town square by the statue. Your loving Father.'

"Well, Saturday morning arrived, the father got up early, eagerly awaiting the time to leave. However, upon approaching the town square he came upon a large crowd of young men, all gathered around the statue, all diligently looking around. Unable to make his way through, he asked a young man standing on the outside what all the commotion was about. Excitedly the young man said his name was . . . Juan . . . and he was responding to an ad his father had placed asking him to come home!"

The man telling the story before the church became silent, a stunned, bittersweet expression etched upon his face. "That South American father never found his son, though he stayed and searched all afternoon . . .

"Max said nothing else upon finishing the story, just left, left me sitting there to see my own stupidity and hardheadedness."

Turning to face his boy, the man discovered his son staring at him with undisguised love. "Needless to say," the man added, "my son and I were reunited."

Spontaneously they hugged each other. Just as spontaneously applause erupted from the listening crowd.

Arm still around his boy's shoulder, he concluded, "I saw Max fairly regularly at the bar after that. We became, I think, friends—good friends."

Four more people spoke for Max, each story moving. But it was the last person's experience that most profoundly affected me—altered my business and personal decision making . . . again.

He was someone I knew of. Very, very wealthy. Very, very successful. His attire alone set him apart from everyone, though his tears united him.

"I, too, learned something from Max, something that affected my whole life deeply, all aspects. He shared a story past President Ronald Reagan told when he was governor of California. It's a story about values.

"Some years ago Bud Wilkinson had one of his great national championship teams in Oklahoma. Toward the end of the season they visited a very mediocre Texas Christian team. Surprisingly that day, TCU exceeded everyone's wildest hopes. In the closing seconds a receiver dived into the end zone to make a ground level catch of what seemed to be the winning touchdown against the national champions. A huge upset was occurring. The crowd went wild. TCU had scored with only seconds left.

"But then, Max told me, way down at the end zone, the

kid who supposedly caught the ball stood up, walked over to the referee and said, 'Sir, the ball hit the ground before I caught it. It's not a touchdown.'

"Then Governor Reagan asked, 'Now, what is your reaction? Do you think the kid went too far with this honesty thing? I mean if the referee didn't see it! Or did you recall all the wrongful calls referees had made to justify yourself?

"'The real question is: if the referee didn't see it, should the player have kept quiet and said nothing?' "After a long thoughtful moment Reagan said, 'Someday that young man may represent you in Congress, or state legislature, or even the White House. Then what? Do you want him to keep his mouth shut if no one is looking? Do you want him to base his decisions on the political notion of "you scratch my back and I'll scratch yours?" Or do you want him to base his decisions on the same kind of internal moral principle that made him tell the truth to the referee in the first place?'

"He closed his talk with this question: 'Who is going to teach our kids those kinds of values if it isn't us?'"

The wealthy man looked around the room. "I don't know if that story did anything for you, but it changed my whole life—it became a blueprint for how I conducted my affairs.

"See, I was raised in a cold, strict family centered around one thing: winning. Winning at all cost. So I became ultra competitive. As a young boy, I'd cheat to win at cards, sports, anything to be first. As you can probably imagine, this disease eventually destroyed my family, friendships, everything, except, of course, my businesses.

"My synchronistically bumping into Max one day altered everything, and I hope I'm a better man, a better husband, father, friend, and business partner because of it."

At that, the man walked briskly out of the church.

Jenny and I stayed in our seats, never getting up to speak. There was no need as others had said it all. We sat holding hands until the church emptied, until no sounds echoed in the still, high cathedral chamber.

❈ ❈ ❈

On our drive home, Jenny brought up the subject of not knowing Max had so many friends, had made such an impact. "Did you know he even knew that many?" she asked.

I shook my head, "Nope. When we were together, it was like we were the only two people in the world . . . Max made it that way, and it always made me feel special."

"He affected me that way too," Jenny replied.

I shared Max's background with her, something I knew now was okay to do because of his death. Before, Max would not have appreciated it.

"The best way to explain where Max came from is to tell you from where his full name originated." I told her what Max had spoken of—the Maxwell Winston Stone bit.

"His early life was bad?" Jenny murmured.

"I think so, though he seldom spoke directly about it."

"What about all his books? Did he really read them all?"

"Yeah, and he didn't start until his mid-thirties . . . He said his reading and learning from the books really changed him . . . actually, he said it radically changed him from who he was early on."

"I've never told you this before, Ross, but besides his healings, it seemed there was a glow, a kind of aura surrounding Max. Did you notice it?"

I looked over at my wife, nodded and sighed deeply. "I never before believed any human could transform as much as Max. If I hadn't seen everything with my own eyes, I wouldn't have believed it."

Jenny smiled, "He truly loved people didn't he?"

Driving became difficult as my eyes teared up remembering this phenomenal man.

CHAPTER SEVENTEEN
Servant As Leader

The stories shared at Max's funeral kept echoing through my mind, along with how little I'd known of my friend's life beyond me. Never would I have guessed he influenced so many, had so many connections.

I had asked him once what he did every day, did he have a routine? He responded by bringing up Albert Schweitzer, the doctor, engineer, musician who lived most of his life under primitive conditions in service to Africans. Another time he quoted from memory John Galsworthy's motto:

"I shall pass through this world but once; any good things, therefore, that I can do, or any kindness I can show to any human being or animal, let me do it now. Let me not defer or neglect, for I shall not pass this way again."

Often I'd hear Max humming the song sung by B.J. Thomas, *He Ain't Heavy, He's My Brother.* I asked him if it was a favorite. Nodding fervently he informed me "Did you know it was about a famous orphanage called Boy's Town? The story goes that an older boy stumbled into the new Boy's Town orphanage carrying a sleeping younger boy on his back. The first official to see them approaching ran up to greet them, saw how exhausted the older boy was and said, 'Let me take the boy off your back, he must be heavy.' Looking confused the older boy said to the official, 'Oh he ain't heavy—he's my brother!'"

Max's stories went straight to the heart, or proved thought provoking. He once posed: "Do you think a servant could be a leader?"

My first impulse was to answer no, a servant would not have the necessary leadership skills. Yet upon thinking more I concluded the opposite: A good leader not only could but should be a servant, a servant to the people he leads. Max's book *Journey to the East* by Herman Hesse heightened my thinking.

"There was once a band of men on an expedition in the Tibetan mountains. All the men," Max explained, "were smart, prominent. All had already achieved great things but still pushed themselves to make some greater discovery.

"One of the hired servants was a man named Leo. At first he did only menial chores, but as the trip became harder he began to sustain them all with his spirit and heart. It seemed this lowly simple servant had a rather extraordinary presence.

"All went well until one day Leo simply disappeared, and all these famous, wealthy men fell apart, their expedition eventually ending. After the breakup, two of the men searched years to find Leo.

"Do you know where he was?" Max asked.

"They discovered Leo in a monastery; actually he was head of the monastery! See this man whom they'd only known as a lowly servant was in fact the leader of many men. Like on their expedition, here too he was the leading light; a great and noble leader."

Max shook his head smiling, "Maybe that's the way all those politicians, our elected leaders are supposed to act, like servants as leaders, rather than the bunch of lowdown, deceiving, lying pack of skunks they are." And he roared with laughter.

✳ ✳ ✳

I pondered this new idea, of leaders being servants. It certainly went against the grain of what we see in everyday politics. In a movie called *Distinguished Gentlemen,* the comedian Eddie Murphy starred as a small-time con man who ran his biggest con of all by running and winning an election to the United States House of Representatives. Arriving in Washington and suddenly hearing about all the money the political action committees were going to give him, he turned to his friend and said, "This is the greatest con in the world—and it's legal!"

Somewhere deep in the vestiges of most humans lies the belief that the leader gets the most and the best, while the followers and servants get less. What if . . . I challenged myself, what if it were that if you wanted to be a leader, you had to become the servant? How would that change this odd, upside-down world we live in?

I love the story of the little boy who, when asked to give blood to his younger sister who badly needed it, solemnly agreed. While the blood transfusion was taking place, the doctor came over to see how the little boy was doing.

Looking up, pale and scared, the boy asked, "How long before I die?"

Wiping the sudden tears from his eyes, the crusty old doctor realized the boy thought he was sacrificing his life in giving blood to save his sister. Gently, he reassured him he would live a long life.

But whoever would be
great among you
must be your servant.
—St. Matthew

CHAPTER EIGHTEEN
Appreciation

Memories of Max would somehow enter my mind at the strangest time. For instance, I was at a closing when one of the discussions we had came to mind.

"Learning to appreciate is an art," Max ranted.

"An art?" I questioned.

"Yep. Being appreciative is a state of mind; it's a way of doing things, an avenue to be developed, a way of life."

Whew! He was really caught up in the topic, and like a whirlwind, I too felt sucked in, spun around and turned inside out. This is what happened being around Max. Everything changed. Nothing remained status quo, for his intensity and focus required an internal revolution. For me, I became more aware of life, especially the common, the ordinary: early morning sunrises, my first cup of coffee, a butterfly flitting into view, a loving gesture from Jenny, a simple smile in the grocery store line. Max transported me out of my unconscious, self-imposed limitation into something new.

Continuing, he told this story:

"A Detroit school teacher specifically requested help from one of her students, a kid named Steve Morris. Do you know why?" Max asked though he didn't wait for an answer. "See this kid had a special hearing ability, probably because he was blind, and she needed help finding a mouse that was disrupting the classroom."

A smile inched upward on Max's lips. "This young boy later recalled it was the first time anyone had ever shown appreciation for his extraordinary, talented hearing ability. He said it was a catalyst for changing his life."

Max grinned, satisfyingly, "From that time forward he developed this gift of hearing, and went on to become . . . " Max paused to enhance the surprise ending, "one of the greatest songwriters and singers of all time, under the stage name of . . . Little Stevie Wonder!"

Again, I found myself awed. And through this story gained more self-knowledge. From it I learned to claim my real gift, something I'd been shamed from doing, and began to appreciate who I was.

❋ ❋ ❋

As I've said before, Max used humor oftentimes to offset seriousness. He balanced one with the other to keep things from becoming too oppressive or judgmental. Like the time he recited what would become my single most favorite poem. It was written anonymously by a Confederate soldier. Max told it to me on a day I was feeling cocky and invincible after making a quick, large profit on a deal. Hearing it toned me down, grounded me once again.

"I asked God for strength,
that I might achieve;
I was made weak, that
I might learn to humbly obey.
I asked for health, that I
might do greater things;
I was given infirmity, that
I might do better things.
I asked for riches,
that I might be happy;
I was given poverty,
that I might be wise.
I asked for power, that I
might have the praise of men;
I was given weakness, that I
might feel the need of God.
I asked for all things,
that I might enjoy life;

I was given life, that I
might enjoy all things.
I got nothing I asked for,
but everything I'd hoped for.
Almost despite myself, my
unspoken prayers were answered.
I am, among all men,
most richly blessed."

You could have heard a butterfly's wings flap upon his finishing. He spoke nothing else. Just let it sink in. Let me ponder it myself.

Then later, to break the solemnity of the mood, he interjected this story. It was told by an old man sitting with other old men around a town square in Texas. At noontime they would gather to talk and sit in the shade. Max began:

"On this particular day the subject matter, unofficially, was fishing. One man really emphasized the importance of being appreciative of everything. With a twinkle in his eyes he told the others a story.

"'One time I was fishing and ran out of bait. Since the fish were biting real good, I didn't want to leave, but also didn't know what I was going to use.

"'Well about that time I happened to look down near my feet and saw a snake carrying a small frog in its mouth. Carefully taking hold of the snake, I gently removed the frog and cut it up for bait.

"'Admittedly, I felt a little bit bad about taking the poor snake's food . . . so to kind of pay him back, I poured a couple drops of my whiskey into its mouth, then returned to my fishing.

"'Well, I continued catching fish with that cut-up frog until I felt something hitting my boot. Looking down, you'll never believe what I saw . . . that same snake, only now he was carrying two more frogs!'"

I genuinely laughed at the punch line, and noticed how much lighter the atmosphere had become. Though the joke was cute, the poem stuck with me the hardest, especially the words: "I asked for riches, that I might be happy. I was given poverty that I might be wise." Little did I know then how profoundly those simple words would intersect with my own life.

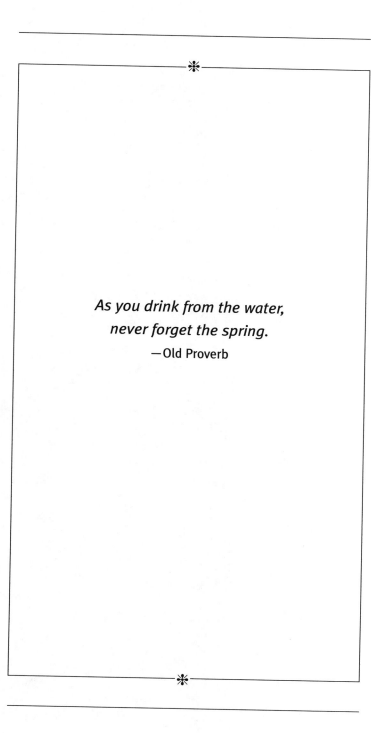

As you drink from the water,
never forget the spring.
—Old Proverb

CHAPTER NINETEEN
Failure Versus Success

Despite the success of my external life, internally I knew I lived a charade, a seductive sham, for in reality fears ruled my life, especially the fear of failing. I recall Max proclaiming one day, "I've never pitched in a World Series game, never played a championship tennis match at Wimbledon, never won a twenty-six-mile marathon race, never received an Oscar for acting, never wrote a best-selling novel.

"Why not?" he indignantly asked. "Because I never even tried. "And in saying this he summed up my life to the core.

I often found myself reminiscing over lost opportunities. My list included baseball, football, writing, theater, even being a veterinarian. All once elicited such interest, all long ago abandoned by perceived inadequacies. "What if?" I pondered too often and bittersweetly before sinking into self-pity or depression's bottomless pit. I hated my weaknesses, but Max's stories and quotes kept me afloat more times than I cared to admit.

But Max kept me focused on success rather than failure through a variety of quotes he intermittently shared, had obviously memorized and interjected whenever he sensed they were needed.

"Ross Jamison," he'd say to me, "listen to these.

"'Never let the fear of striking out get in your way,' Babe Ruth." Or, "'Men are born to succeed, not to fail,' Henry David Thoreau.

"Don't forget," Max would remind me, "the best hitters in professional baseball have batting averages of only .300 to .400. That means, even the greatest hitters fail six or seven times out of ten!

"Don't mix up what you do, or how well it's done, with your value as a human. Your true value comes from within, not from any external accomplishment."

Or, "Remember the turtle; he makes progress only when he sticks his neck out."

At another time when I was obsessing over a failure in some new venture, Max again pulled out that overloaded, jam-packed wallet. "Listen to this," he spoke. "At age twenty-two he failed in business. Ran for the legislature at twenty-three, but was defeated at the polls. He embarked on another business venture at twenty-four, and failed again. He was finally elected to the legislature at the age of twenty-five, but his sweetheart died and he had a nervous breakdown at twenty-seven. He ran for speaker of the house at twenty-nine, elector at thirty-one, and for Congress at thirty-four, each and every time defeated at the polls. He was eventually elected to the Congress at age thirty-seven, but defeated again at thirty-nine. At forty-six he was defeated for vice president, at forty-nine he was again defeated for the Senate, but at the age of fifty-one was elected President of the United States."

"President?" I questioned.

Max roared, "Abraham Lincoln!"

"You're kidding me?"

"Nope. So don't be so damned all afraid of making a mistake. Even if you did, you'd be in the best of company!"

I remembered shaking my head in amazement, then unable to suppress a slow, spreading smile asked, "Hey, with all this wisdom how come you aren't some big, famous, successful guy?"

Eyes as innocent as a baby, they peered directly into mine, "Oh, I am my friend, I think I am."

❋　❋　❋

At the time, I was oblivious as to how all of these little bits of wisdom Max shared would soon be put to an excruciating, painful, Herculean test.

CHAPTER TWENTY
A New Value Put Into Practice

All of Max's stories, generosity, humor and close friendship coalesced as preparation for the most difficult, monumental decision I'd ever make. Like a viral infection, its consequences spread rapidly and infected every aspect of my life: the relationship with my wife, our home, business partners, friendships, church, community, everything. The world shook itself, turned inside out and left me frightened to the core.

✳   ✳   ✳

The day began seemingly normal. A potential new business opportunity crossed my desk, like so many others. It looked simple. Easy. Innocent at first.

The deal was this. A man with whom I'd participated in another highly profitable real estate transaction put it together. He told me of a connection he'd developed with two people highly placed in the Department of Transportation for the state of Colorado, and in the Corps of Engineers. For some heavy "inducement money" to these two individuals, he could get a certain piece of land condemned, which we would then purchase from the state for pennies on the dollar. Furthermore, he'd already lined up a buyer for the property with financing all in place.

It looked good. Great in fact. Since I knew the person who brought it to me fairly well, trusted him reasonably well, and because my downside loss would be limited to only $125,000—versus an upside potential profit of over $2,000,000—I figured it a no-brainer.

What I didn't know at the time were the current owners: that they'd owned the land for three generations, were good people, and though poor, had already rejected umpteen offers to buy their property, which sat smack dab in the middle of prime development. I knew nothing of the struggles each of the three generations had in order to keep their land, nor of their current desperation to continue holding on to it. None of this I knew at the onset. I discovered it way late into the highly profitable venture.

I couldn't see a way to stop it. Other people were involved behind the scenes; too many high-profile, well-connected power brokers had their hand in the pie. And unless I wanted to turn against my partners and these other people causing them to lose terrific sums of money, forfeit my $125,000, lose my reputation and even more important open us all up to lawsuits and liabilities that could easily wipe us out, I'd have to keep quiet, go along with the crowd.

For a while things went well. I maintained the status quo. Certainly I had doubts, but successfully squashed them each time they reared up. That is, until an interruption from my secretary. Someone was on the telephone, a guy who'd called fifteen or twenty times, mostly screaming, sometimes crying. Would I please talk to him?

Intuitively, I sensed I shouldn't take this call. But I did anyway. Picking up the telephone, I quickly learned how ruinous our land acquisition was going to be. I saw how real people were involved, were being hurt. People who had names, were powerless and obviously were unjustifiably being screwed. After what seemed an eternity, I took his number, told him I'd think on it, hung up, and saw my life turn into a living hell.

It consumed me totally; occupied my every waking thought, which was all the time, as sleep became impossible. Confused and frightened, I continued to ask myself, How could I kill the deal? How could I choose to lose everything? How could I make a decision that would not only financially break me, but would ostracize me from my own business community?

I rationalized. Tried lying to myself. Ran through every possible scenario. Cried. Stamped my feet. Told myself it wasn't fair, it was too hard of a decision to make—tried everything. But nothing worked. Nothing felt right . . . except one thing . . . so . . . I pulled the plug. Killed the deal, and all hell broke loose.

Oddly I felt as if Max were with me, by my side, never trying to persuade me either way, always allowing me to make my own decision.

✳   ✳   ✳

I was ruined, plus now was viewed as a pariah in my own community. On the positive side: The family still owned their land, but unfortunately was suing everyone involved for a fortune.

I lost everything. Almost. Everything except a small sum of money the landowners allowed me, which would keep my wife and me modestly comfortable. We had to sell our huge house for a smaller one, and sold our expensive automobiles for less expensive ones, along with the art and antiques and jewelry . . .

Did I regret my decision?

At times, no doubt. But they were short-lived. Mostly I remembered Max's saying, "Success is not measured by how much money someone makes, or the position they attain. Real success is measured by how a person sleeps at night; if a man can look himself in the eyes when he shaves; what his family thinks of him; how he feels when alone, or when praying. These are the things of real value," he'd say, "things even death can't take away."

✳ ✳ ✳

I have a confession to make: last night I slept like a baby; this morning looked directly into my own eyes while shaving; my wife said she's proud of me; and when I'm alone, I make good company! But then what else should I expect? I had a good teacher.

The image that frequently crosses my mind, what I had written on Max's tombstone, will forever be etched in my memory. I hope he wouldn't mind:

In Memory of
Maxwell W. Stone
1925–1999
Loved By His Son
Ross Jamison

CHAPTER TWENTY-ONE
Slowing Down

Life is slower now. No hustle and bustle. No meetings. No racing somewhere, then back again. It's like a rebirth; like a second life; another chance. I feel new—fresh.

And simple things have emerged, things I'd stopped seeing, seldom appreciated. Now they magically blossom before me. Flowers. Trees. The warm sun. Butterflies, lady-bugs, children and their uninhibited squeals of delight. Smells. Touching. Sleep. Life cycles. Friends. My wife. Movies. Books. Long walks.

This morning Jenny said she loved me, right out of the blue, that I was the bravest man she'd ever known. Then she cried.

I cried too, and felt grand.

I've been thinking of that poem Max shared. I don't know why I recalled it. But I do, word-for-word, and know I'll never forget it. I hear Max speaking the words as if he were beside me now:

"I asked God for strength,
that I might achieve,
I was made weak, that I
might learn to humbly obey.
I asked for health,
that I might do greater things,
I was given infirmity,
that I might do better things.
I asked for riches,
that I might be happy,
I was given poverty,
that I might be wise.
I asked for power, that I might
have the praise of men,
I was given weakness that I might
feel the need of God.
I asked for all things,
that I might enjoy all things,
I got nothing that I asked for—
But everything I had hoped for.

Almost despite myself, my unspoken
Prayers were answered.
I am, among all men and women,
Most richly blest."

✳ ✳ ✳

I've almost completed the monumental task of unpacking Max's books. It took a while before I could start, before I could even look at them. But the time has finally arrived. His books now fill the entire basement, all resting in new floor-to-ceiling bookshelves I have built. I find a spot for the last book by squeezing it tightly in between two others. Viewing the sheer quantity, I shake my head in amazement over Max's incredible feat.

Walking over to the first shelf, I pick one up, sit down, open to the first page and begin reading. I mean if Max had done it, so can I . . . especially now that I have all the time in the world.

CHAPTER TWENTY-TWO
The Last Healing

There is something about Max I haven't shared with you. I thought you might not be able to handle it just yet. I think you are ready now. It concerns the third healing by Max that I observed—one even greater than the other two.

Jenny, Max and I had just left the Denver Performing Arts Complex on Fourteenth Street. Returning to our car, we heard the sudden shrill shriek of tires squealing, followed by shouts. Right next to us, we witnessed a van slamming into a young boy who had obviously bolted into the street. We watched the terrified father run out to pick up his son who had been thrown some fifteen feet. As we approached, he was stroking his small son's head and sobbing uncontrollably.

It was easy to see the child was dead. A bystander tried to resuscitate him, but as soon as he touched the boy's chest, he suddenly stopped and lowered his head.

"Oh God, no, please don't do this to me, please don't!" the boy's father pleaded over and over.

Turning toward Max, I observed the quickening glow around his head. With no hesitation, he walked directly over to the man, whispered something in his ear and picked up the boy. Holding, loving, comforting the small body, we all observed a faint golden aura, growing and surrounding both Max and the boy.

Everyone stood transfixed, as if time had come to a standstill, awed by the light, all sensing something rare about to occur.

Then it happened. First, the boy coughed. Then cried out for his father.

A cheer rose. And everyone was crying, especially Jenny and me. More so, Max.

People swarmed toward Max as he handed the boy back to the stunned father. They began asking to be healed, or to heal a friend or family member. Questions echoed everywhere. Light bulbs flashed.

Quickly, Max ran to us and yelled, "We'd best get out of here."

A taxi was waiting for patrons from the play so we hailed it and drove away with many of the people running after us.

By the next morning, somehow Max's address had been identified, and his small apartment yard swarmed with news people and fanatic extremists proclaiming he was a false god. In total, Max's life became so miserable we had to sneak him over to stay in our home until the hype slowed down.

More than anything else, Max was embarrassed over the publicity and attention thrown at him, both the positive and the negative. He hated not being able to be what he was—a storyteller.

"Now," he complained to me, "no one wants to hear my stories anymore—now they all want . . . or demand . . . to be healed . . . to part the waters . . . or have manna rain down from heaven."

✳ ✳ ✳

Before he died, and after the evening following Max's third healing, the three of us were sitting out in our backyard drinking Jenny's special recipe for iced tea. It was delicious.

Max began. "I know you've been wondering how I do the healings."

Jenny and I both sat forward in our chairs.

"I still don't fully understand, or adequately know how to explain it . . . It's like the injuries are an illusion, and

I just break through them, kind of clear our visions . . . Can you follow that?"

"Not really," I murmured while Jenny shook her head no.

"Let me try another approach," Max volunteered. "This is something very, very sacred, though it may be difficult to understand at first . . . that which is real, can never be harmed; that which is unreal, doesn't exist."

Jenny and I both repeated the words to ourselves, yet remained perplexed.

"Okay," Max said thoughtfully, "This is the most important thing I can tell you.

"Inside you is all the inner knowledge from the past . . . You may recall what Christ did when the Pharisees and Scribes brought the adulterous woman to him. They cited that the law of Moses commanded she be stoned and asked what Jesus thought. He then did something really peculiar; he bent down and wrote with his fingers on the ground. Eventually he stood and made the one statement, which blew the Pharisees out of the water, 'Let him who is without sin be the first to throw a stone at her!'

"Do you see? By bending downward writing on the ground, he was removing himself from the physical, the external, and went inside himself, to his secret closet within, and received the knowledge of what to say."

"Max," I questioned. "I didn't know you had even read the Bible."

"Oh, you bet I have," he retorted, "quite thoroughly, but let's continue.

"Did you know we are so busy dealing with everyday matters, we have forgotten that which is within us has the greatest powers?

"People only use seven to ten percent of their brains. And to utilize a greater amount, we are going to have to develop the inner dimensions.

"We can't trust our physical senses to give us a true understanding of reality because the physical senses lie to us with such fantastic tales we choose to believe them."

This time both of our heads nodded yes. Though I had never heard this knowledge before, somehow it felt familiar.

Max's face strained with intention. "If we continue to identify with our outer egos alone, we will cut ourselves off from our inner abilities . . . This is one of the meanings of Christ's statement, 'Whoever seeks his life shall lose it, and whoever loses his life will gain it'. . . See, he means those who seek only the external, ego side will miss the inner, but those who shrug off the outer world, who seek the inner, will find a much richer and more powerful life."

He paused, and then added with great emphasis.

"This is why I am able to heal, and why anyone can. Even you."

I remembered involuntarily gulping, then felt a shudder run through my body.

To be continued . . .

EPILOGUE

The Native American Lakota people tell the story of a white buffalo-calf woman who brought them their sacred pipe. When asked by a reporter if the story was true, one of the Lakota elders replied, "Well, I don't know whether it actually happened or not, but you can see for yourself that it's true."

This is the same task you as a reader have in deciding if the stories you have just read are true or not. Like the Lakota elder spoke, only you can determine a story's veracity, regardless if it ever happened or not.

BIBLIOGRAPHICAL NOTE

I have collected the parables and stories in this book over a period of many years. Several of them have a history of having been passed from one person to another and are to my knowledge not attributed to any one person. The sources for the stories I do know are listed below.

CHAPTER 1

The parable of two men traveling on a road can be found in the book by John Hick titled *Faith and Knowledge* (1988).

CHAPTER 2

The quote from the Sean Penn interview is attributed to Joni Mitchell and can be found on the Sean Penn homepage,

http://www.geocities.com/Hollywood/Bungalow/
6339/Entertainment

CHAPTER 15

The story *The Hundredth Monkey* is in a book by the same title by Ken Keys, Jr. (1984).

CHAPTER 16

The poem titled "The Guy in the Glass" appeared in an Ann Landers column under the title "The Man in the Glass." It was written by Dale Wimbrow and was first published under the title "The Guy in the Glass" in *American Magazine* (1934).

The story of the father searching for his son is a common theme in sermons on relationships and can be traced back to a short story, "The Capital of the World," by Ernest Hemingway. It can be found in *The Fifth Column* and the *First Forty-Nine Stories* (1938).

CHAPTER 17

The story of the little boy giving blood appears in the book *Chicken Soup for the Soul* by Jack Canfield and Mark Victor Hansen (1984). A similar story (with a little girl giving blood) was portrayed in a 1925 movie *Little Annie Rooney,* starring Mary Pickford.

To catch a glimpse of the future, read

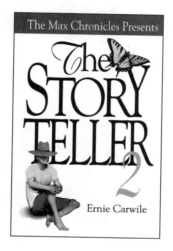

BOOK ORDERS

To purchase more copies of *STORYTELLER I*

2 copies or less	$14.95 ea.
3–10 copies	$11.95 ea.
Volume Discount	For orders of 10 or more call for price

To purchase more copies of *STORYTELLER II*

2 copies or less	$14.95 ea.
3–10 copies	$11.95 ea.
Volume Discount	For orders of 10 or more call for price

Order Books:

1. Send a check to
   Verbena Pond Publishing Co., LLC
   P.O. Box 370270
   Denver, CO 80237

2. Order through PayPal on our website:
   www.thestoryteller1.com

3. Fax your credit card number, expiration date,
   your name and address to our toll free number:
   1-866-488-3196.